We All Fall

Helen Vivienne Fletcher

Copyright

For Jess - thank you for always being the sanity that
lives outside my body.

Chapter One

The air was still the day she arrived. We'd spent weeks battling a strange, hot summer wind, the big top closed several nights as flapping tent sides turned to thundering, drowning out the music and scaring the punters. There were no creatures to spook, of course. Those days long gone as animal-cruelty had been replaced with long hours of training human bodies to complete impossible feats.

Not that *I* did impossible feats these days, unless you counted reviving well-worn, ripped costumes and sewing sparkles in the minimal light of early morning. The world often had a pink shine to it when I opened my eyes – the result of rogue sequins stuck to my eyelashes. I'd let my hair grow long since I'd stopped performing, as I no longer had to tame it into a bun each day. The wild and wiry curls claimed the sparkles too. No matter how often I washed my hair, there was always a shimmer to it, and a few sequins falling from my shoulders to leave a trail behind me wherever I went. I swore they were sentient, breeding and moving when I wasn't looking.

We all watched as the new caravan rolled in. The fortune teller's tent was already set up, waiting for them. It had been months since we'd had a psychic travel with us. The last one had taken her role a little too seriously and gone mad with the visions she saw.

1

I was supposed to be in the costume room, fixing one of the clown's suspenders. Apparently, it wasn't so funny if her pants fell down when it wasn't planned.

I'd snuck out when I'd heard the rumour of their arrival whispered around the tents. The caravan door opened, and an older woman wafted out. She was draped in a black lace shawl with an impractical fringe. If I hadn't already heard the talk, I would have mistaken her for the teller. Instead, I waited, holding my breath, for the girl to appear.

"Myra, what are you doing?!"

I spun around at the sound of my mother's voice. I lost my balance as I did, sprawling in the dirt.

My mother stepped back, wincing at the sight of me. It looked strange on her. She was always so poised; her glittering stage make up and perfect bun replacing her real skin and hair almost constantly. Negative facial expressions broke the effect and were therefore rarely allowed.

I pulled myself up onto my hands and knees, wincing too at the never-ending tenderness in my right leg. "I wanted to see her arrive," I said.

My mother didn't reply, her attention seemingly taken by something just over my shoulder. I knew there was nothing there; she just couldn't bear to look at me. I hadn't seen her eyes meet mine since the day of my accident.

She nodded absently, accepting the explanation, or perhaps simply acknowledging that I had stopped talking. She held out a leotard. "I need this fixed for tonight."

I sighed, glancing back towards the teller's caravan. The door was closed, the girl already inside the tent.

My mother followed my gaze and smiled slightly. "I'm sure you'll get a chance to meet Giselle later. Maybe you can even get a reading."

I scowled. "I don't believe in psychics."

My mother chuckled. "Well, perhaps she doesn't believe in trapeze artists."

"It's a good thing I'm not one of those, then." My tone was harsh, and I watched her face fall. Her eyes flicked towards my leg, then she closed them, a shudder working its way up her body.

"Don't let anyone hear you say you don't believe in the teller," she said, her voice flat. "We must always–"

"Keep up the show," I finished for her.

She nodded, her expression tired, suddenly. She turned to head back to her rehearsal, then paused. "Do you need any help getting up?" she asked.

I thought of the pain I would feel, once my weight was back on my feet, and the wobbling uncertainty of those first few steps. A hand – an arm to link through – would ease some of that, making me feel safer.

"No, I'm fine on my own," I said.

She nodded curtly, then walked away. I waited until she was out of sight before biting my lip and pulling myself to my feet.

I DON'T KNOW IF IT was a sign of a lack of parental bond that led my mother and father to send me flying through the air. Maybe it was a misguided belief that the bond was so strong it could conquer gravity. Either way, gravity had won. My leg had shattered in three places, and my feet had been firmly on the ground ever since.

I didn't mind. Well, of course I minded the lingering pain and the limp that made me question every step. But I liked my new role working on the costumes. Not so much the mending, but when I had the chance to make something from scratch. I liked being able to create something that's beauty would last longer than the fleeting moment of thrill my tricks in the air had been. It was a chance to put my own ideas and design into the world, rather than just repeating the same choreography my parents had come up with over and over.

I finished mending the suspender and my mother's costume as quickly as I could, hoping I would have a chance to catch a glimpse of Giselle before the gates opened to the public that night, but by the time I'd attached the last sequin, there were already hoards milling around outside her tent, curious about the new attraction. I knew she wouldn't get a chance to step outside until the night was done.

I walked down to the smoko area as my parents' act began. My mother wanted me to watch their routine each night. To "keep it fresh" in my mind. She was still deluding herself that my injury would heal, and I would be returning to join them someday. I couldn't stay in the big top, though, not even to make her happy. If I watched them flip and twirl one more time, my leg wouldn't be the only thing that snapped.

I took my home-school work with me, settling down with my books in front of the trashcan fire. I was hoping to finish another assignment and send it away in the morning. The workers sitting on their breaks were rowdy, but they mostly left me out of it. They were hardly the most polite when it came to women, but they either felt harassing a fifteen year old was going too far, or they were scared stiff of my father's right hook, powered by years of the most intense upper body workout the circus had to offer. Of course, the performers avoided me too, the superstitious fear of someone who'd fallen keeping them away.

"Hey, Myra."

I glanced up as Luca sat down next to me. I hesitated, then closed my book, welcoming his company. At seventeen, he was the closest to my age in our traveling family. He was a performer, but he was a sceptic through and through and made a hobby of tempting fate just to watch the superstitious ones squirm.

"You met the new girl, yet?" he asked.

I shook my head. He obviously held the same hope I did, that another person our age would bring some sense of youth back to our lives.

He grinned. "You think she knows she's entering the land of the damned?"

I laughed. "Got to be damned already to come here." Making exhibits out of body abnormalities was no longer politically correct, but the circus was still full of freaks either way.

"If I were her, I'd be running in the other direction."

I reached out, touching Luca's arm to quiet him. He had been saying things like that a lot recently. If he wasn't careful, leaving wouldn't be his choice anymore. The ringmaster did not take kindly to complaints.

He took a breath, letting go of his frustration. His face softened as he took my hand from his arm and squeezed it. I'd left a sparkle on his shoulder. He would flick it off when he saw it.

I could see another glinting in amongst his dark curls. I ran my hand through his hair, plucking it out.

His eyelids fluttered as I did, and he opened his mouth to speak, but I handed him the sequin before he could.

"A present for you," I said.

He laughed and took the sparkle from me, pressing it to the back of his hand. "I'm always covered in these after I hang out with you." He often complained about me leaving my marks on him.

"I saw her mother," I told him, bringing the conversation back to the subject which had been occupying my thoughts all evening. "Bathed in faux-mystique. If the teller's anything like her, they'll be raking it in."

Luca shook his head. "Another mother-daughter pair, eh?"

Luca nudged my side, and I forced a laugh to avoid the moment becoming awkward. Though he was jaded now, and perhaps regretting the decision, he had joined the circus of his own volition. He couldn't understand what it was like to be born into it. I wondered if Giselle felt the same way I did about growing up like this. It would be hard to say, given I was never sure from one day to the next how I felt about it myself.

"You hear she's blind?" Luca asked.

I shrugged. "You think it's for real?" I'd heard the rumours, but no one seemed sure whether it was true or just part of the act. There was an added layer of mystery to a young girl telling fortunes by feel alone. Even the most sceptical had to find that interesting. Curiosity had always been the main draw of the circus. The crowds gathered to catch a glimpse of a world – of people – that didn't quite match up to the rules of their own.

Luca sighed. "I think it's an act," he said. "Gotta know by now, none of this is real."

"So cynical, Luca. Where's your sense of wonder at the show?" I tried to keep a straight face as I quoted our ringmaster's familiar pep talk.

Luca shook his head. "There's no wonder here, Myra. Sleight-of-hand magic, threats of danger all carefully controlled to be perfectly safe ..." He trailed off, and I could tell he'd suddenly remembered my snapped safety line.

His pity filled the space between us, coating both of us thicker than grease paint. I felt my face heat up and I turned to the fire, as if I could pass it off as warmth from the flames.

He cleared his throat. "I'm sorry. I didn't mean–"

"Hey, it's okay," I said quickly. "Nothing's ever perfect, not even safety, right?"

"Right."

We didn't mention the growing number of accidents that had happened recently. None of the others had been as catastrophic as mine – most were simple slips, failures of props or sets, leaving performers with sprained ankles or bruises to ice. We'd blamed the weather – the heartless wind that had been raking its way through all of us and shaking us in more ways than one, but there was no denying the wind wasn't the only thing to blame. There were some in the group who thought I'd brought a curse down on all of us the moment I dropped from that platform into nothing.

"I don't think she's lying," I said.

"Huh?" Luca's thoughts had wandered, and it took him a moment to return to me and our discussion of Giselle.

"The new girl. I think she's really blind."

Luca gave another shrug. "Could be. Guess we'll find out."

I gazed into the fire, letting my eyes soften. I didn't bother to try explaining it to Luca, but I wanted it to be true that she was blind. I couldn't even entirely explain it to myself, but I felt like something would change for me if she were.

Chapter Two

I decided to take my mother's suggestion to go get a fortune from Giselle. She wouldn't know that I was a freak – one of the circus folk – so I would get to see what she was like when performing and fooling the normals, unless she really was psychic, of course, but I didn't believe it. In that department, I was just as cynical as Luca.

I didn't get the chance for the first few days. The excitement of a new attraction had brought in a new boon of punters, and the ringmaster had added more matinees. I was kept busy mending and making new costumes for the daytime alternate performers. Even if I hadn't been, there was no way I would have been able to get the chance for a reading. Word had spread of the new fortune teller's strangely accurate work, and lines of people circled her tent as if they planned to strangle it.

For three days, all I saw were glimpses of her. A small peek through the gauzy curtains as one customer left, and another entered the tent. Those stolen glances only gave me a fleeting impression. She had long blonde hair, which draped her face, obscuring it from my viewpoint, and she wore appropriately mystical sweeping clothing. The effect was of someone shrouded from the world, swaddled in enough layers to keep her safe... or to keep the world safe from her. Perhaps the layers were supposed to hold the magic in.

Each time I peeked, I saw her mother hovering in the tent too. I didn't know her role in the act. The child psychic was the draw card; the lace-draped mother just seemed to be a power-hungry add on. Of course, I was bringing my own damage into that thought. My mother may as well have hovered over every flying leap I'd made before my fall.

I took to spending my evenings, once the late performances had started and the other tents had closed down, walking on a loop that took me past her tent. Or limping in a loop, rather. I would get slower and less steady as the evening wore on, the pain growing with each step. Somehow, I couldn't make myself stop though. Passing her tent wasn't the intention, of course. I had no desire to stalk the girl, but I found myself drawn back there each night.

Finally, on the afternoon of the fourth day, a lull in the crowd outside her tent coincided with my finishing my mending. I hovered, unsure whether or not to go in. Her lace-cloaked mother caught sight of me and beckoned me forward.

"Don't be shy, dear, the spirits welcome all." Her voice quavered, a poor attempt at creating mystique.

I suppressed a smile and made my way between the swathes of brightly-coloured and bejewelled fabric curtaining the entrance. A strong smell of incense greeted me, though I couldn't see any burning.

"Sit down." She gestured grandly to a stool perched in front of a small table covered by a lace tablecloth much resembling the shawl she wore. "Giselle will be with you shortly."

The interior of the tent was partitioned off by more of the gauzy, colourful fabric and lit only with candlelight. She slipped between one of those partitions, leaving me seemingly alone.

Though I'd never worked the fortune teller's tent, I knew enough of the tricks of the trade to guess that they were watching me now, observing my body language and making educated guesses about me. I sat down on the stool wondering what it was I was telling them.

A tap against the floor made me turn. Her mother held the swathes of fabric back as Giselle came forward. I saw now why I'd never been able to see her face, earlier. She wore a white veil covering her eyes, hanging to just above her lips. She felt her way forward, tapping a white stick back and forth to guide her. I frowned as she bumped a table, the candle on top of it shuddering, threatening to fall. The drapes and candles seemed a dangerous mix given the circumstances.

Her stumbling, unsteady progress reminded me of my own unsure steps. Just like me, each careful footstep was an act of faith, bravado and fear. But she crossed the room safely, coming to sit opposite me. She took a deep breath, and I found myself doing the same. It was strangely calming to match my inhales and exhales to hers.

She held out her hands. "Please."

I hesitated, then placed my hands in hers.

She ran her thumb along the lines of my right palm. It tickled, and I had to resist the urge to pull away. Her palms were cool, and she sat calmly, at one with the supposed spirits surrounding her.

"You wish to see the future," she said. Her voice was low and steady, none of the forced drama her mother had feigned.

I shrugged, then realised that was not an answer I could give when she couldn't see the movement. "I saw the tent," I said, still not admitting to working here. "It seemed interesting."

She nodded. "The future always draws us." She turned to business then, dropping the mystique a little. "It's five dollars for a fortune, ten for a *good* fortune and twelve for a fortune and a wish."

I frowned. I'd heard others mention the teller's strange method of charging double to only hear the positive parts of what she saw. I'd assumed it was a joke, but here she was offering me the chance to tint the future in a rosy glow.

She smiled, recognising my confusion without having to see it. "It's very rare you can change the course of the future. Why hear the bad stuff if you can't do anything about it?"

"I don't believe in psychics." I surprised myself with the bluntness of my words. I hadn't meant to tell her that, but something about the setting made my natural guards drop away and honesty slip out.

"I'm not a psychic," she said. "I just tell fortunes."

I puzzled over the difference. She didn't seem offended by my words, and she didn't ask why I had come if I didn't believe, perhaps having seen this all too often. I reached into my pocket, sorting the coins stashed there. I had eleven dollars, enough to ask her to edit out the things I didn't want to hear. Curiosity made me want her to tell me everything though, and I knew choosing the good fortune would mean spending the night sleepless, wondering about the parts she'd withheld. Even though I didn't believe it was real, I still wanted to hear her whole prediction.

I placed five dollars in her hand. "Just a fortune," I said.

She tilted her head slightly. "You're a brave one."

She said it like a statement of fact, and I couldn't tell whether she was praising or making fun of me. She left her hand lingering on mine, and I felt my breath quicken, a strange warmth starting in my stomach. It spread to my cheeks, making me light-headed. I drew my hand away.

She was still for a moment then folded her hand over the money. "I'll give you the wish for free," she said. "Circus-worker discount."

I gaped at her, and her lips curled up, smirking at my surprise.

"I bet I'll have seen every one of you enter my tent by the time we're done here." It was an off-hand comment, but something about her tone made it sound ominous.

She took out a pack of tarot cards, spreading them across the small table. I watched, fascinated by the beautiful artwork. Each was painted in dark purples and blues, with flecks of silver catching the light and bringing the designs to life. Swirling patterns surrounded the figures on each card.

She laid them out – Le Chariot, La Roue De Fortune, Le Diable, L'Amoureux, La Lune ...

I blinked as the last card seemed to move, the image coming alive and twisting under my gaze. The silver flecks flashed, and Giselle jerked her hand away, dropping the card as if it was burning. Her breath caught, then she hesitated, her fingers hovering just above the cards.

"Did that just ...?" I trailed off, realising I couldn't ask her if she'd seen what I'd seen. I shook my head, trying to clear it.

The images on the cards were motionless now. Their patterns colourful but two dimensional. A trick of the light and my own exhaustion, I told myself. But still I found my gaze flicking back to the card, checking for movement. Sweat crept down my temples, as I waited for her to speak.

Giselle's mother cleared her throat. I started and glanced at the lace-cloaked figure in the corner of the room. I'd forgotten she was there, hovering and watching. Now that I'd become aware of her, her presence was hard to dismiss.

Giselle shook herself slightly and returned to spreading the cards. "The spirits have a lot to say tonight, it seems."

I shivered as she began to tell me my fortune, but her words were fairly generic. Be wary of strangers entering your life ... the wind will bring with it big changes and trials ... There was nothing specific and nothing to make me rethink my position on psychics.

I brushed the perspiration from my forehead and tried to concentrate, but my interest was gone, and it was a struggle to keep my focus from wandering around the room.

Finally, she gathered the cards together, patting them into line between her hands. "If you have any final questions for the spirits, ask them now."

"No," I said. "Thank you," I added, not wanting to sound rude.

She cocked her head slightly, surprised by the speed of my refusal. I watched for any more movement from the cards, but there was nothing. They were just a prop, I had decided, and not a terribly well-thought-out one either. Whether the blindness was part of her act or not, it meant she couldn't read the cards. Instead she just shifted them back and forth, making pretty patterns with no meaning.

"Not a single question. Perhaps not so brave after all."

This time I was certain she was making fun of me.

"Make your wish tonight," she said. "It must be the last thing you think about before you fall asleep."

I'd forgotten about the wish and her circus-worker discount. I wondered again what had given me away – what had outed me as part of the circus. I could have asked her, but then I would have had to admit I'd been trying to fool her by coming here without announcing myself properly. I suppose it didn't matter either way, but I'd wanted to be able to pass for normal, even if it was just for one night.

She tilted her head again, as if she were thinking. "Lavender," she said finally.

"Huh?"

She smiled. "That's your flower. You must sleep with some under your pillow. Mother, do we have any?" Giselle turned, her head vaguely aimed towards the corner where her mother stood.

Her mother nodded, grandly, and stepped towards the gap in the drapes. "A beautiful offering, my dear. I'm sure that will please the spirits greatly." She slipped through the opening, disappearing into the depths of the tent.

I made to stand, really wanting to leave rather than wait for a sprig of some flower I wasn't sure I even liked, but Giselle grabbed my arm before I could.

"Be careful, Myra," she whispered. "The spirits have taken a liking to you."

"How do you know my name?" I tried to pull away, but she gripped me tighter.

She shook her head, fiercely. "They saw you fall," she hissed. "They wanted to claim you, but you cheated death. They don't like to be cheated."

"Wh-what?" I couldn't help the stutter forcing its way through my lips.

She pulled me closer, pressing her cheek to mine and whispered. "We must fight them, you and I. They want to cause us to fail. We must fight them, or we will all fall."

She released my arm, sinking suddenly into the chair. I sat frozen, too scared to move. Her mother wafted back into the room, the scent of the lavender trailing after her.

Giselle didn't speak again, her head drooping under the veil as if exhaustion had overcome her.

Her mother pressed the lavender into my hand. "Under your pillow, dear," she quavered. "It will make the wish that much stronger."

Giselle didn't speak again, and I felt her mother's hand on my shoulder, urging me to stand and guiding me towards the door.

I stumbled out. Afternoon had turned to evening while I was in the tent, but the temperature hadn't dropped any. For once, I wished for the feeling of the wind whipping against my face; something to cool my burning cheeks. I wondered whether we were, in fact, cursed. We had gone from the damaging wind to a thick, damp heat, both of which left us begging for air, or rain, or just anything to break the tension.

There were still hordes of people milling about the grounds. It seemed strange. There was a quiet to the teller's tent, the noise dampened somehow. Coming out into the intensity of people and light felt wrong.

I searched for Luca, wanting someone to share the experience with, someone to hug me and bring me back to the real, solid, earth-bound world. But one glance inside the big top showed me he was working. He was covering one of the concession stands, one of his most hated jobs. But still he played the part with joking banter, and the occasional moment of flirting when it was right for the customer. I could see the strain behind his smile, and the lack of energy in his laugh.

He caught my eye, spotting me as I hovered half-in, half-out of the doorway. His smile turned genuine, but it lasted only briefly. He made a face and mimed something to me. I wasn't sure what the individual gestures meant, but I got the gist as "so busy, will see you tomorrow".

I shrugged and nodded my assent back. Without Luca, there was no one else I wanted to talk to. Behind him, I could see my father's strong upside-down hands swinging back and forth, back and forth, waiting for my mother to leap into them. I could go in and watch, but the thought made a sickening shudder work its way up from my stomach to my throat. The ground seemed to tilt beneath me every time I even thought about heights, let alone watching my parents swing in them. I walked away and wandered around the grounds instead, avoiding the teller's tent this time.

The smell of lavender trailed after me. Every few minutes I would catch the scent of it as I inhaled, and Giselle's words would float back into my mind. I thought of tossing the flower, but somehow, I couldn't bring myself to do it.

The incense smoke had permeated my clothes too, making my throat tickle with a cough that wouldn't form. I took to breathing shallowly, just to avoid the sensory assault, until I got dizzy and my head started to pound.

I returned to my caravan, craving the silence and softness of my bed. Despite my reservations, I did place the lavender under my pillow, following the instructions I'd been given. I lay my head down, once more breathing in the natural perfume.

I couldn't clear my head enough to wish, though. No matter what I did, all I could think about was her.

Chapter Three

I still felt unsettled the next morning. I ignored the piles of costumes I had waiting for mending and skipped breakfast in favour of going for a walk. The pain in my leg began to scream, protesting against the amount of pacing I had done lately, and I found myself limping back towards the smoko spot as a place to rest.

Luca was there, waiting for me after not being able to talk last night. He grinned as he saw me, and I smiled, happy to have the distraction.

He took my hand, helping me to a seat, then sat down next to me. His arm was pressed against mine and I frowned at the closeness. The warmth of his skin was too much now the days of wind had finally stilled.

"Did you hear there was another fall last night?"

I shook my head. I had been asleep when my parents came back, but it's not like they would have told me anyway. They both tended to avoid mentioning anything that came too close to the subject of my accident.

"How bad?"

"Worst since yours. She'll be okay though."

I didn't ask who it was. In all honesty, I didn't care. By this point, it seemed like it didn't matter. We had all either fallen or would probably be the next to drop. Each name whispered around the grounds, joining the list of the unfortunate.

"So, you went to see the teller last night?"

I let out a short, humourless laugh. We were all so starved for entertainment; any simple act could become gossip. I had been desperate to tell him about it, last night, but today in the daylight, I felt too silly. Luca would scoff the moment I mentioned spirits, and he wouldn't believe me about the shifting patterns on the cards.

"She plays her role well," I said instead.

Luca nodded. "Don't we all." There was a bitterness to his words. He'd grown bored with his routines long ago, but there was no other part for him to move into, other than filling in on odd jobs like the concession stand last night. The rest of the time, he was stuck in an impish act, welcoming and teasing guests with a few simple stunts as they made their way into the show. It was better than the concessions but not by much.

"Is she really blind?" he asked.

I frowned, replaying the events of the night before in my head and trying to work out whether I knew the answer. If she wasn't, the act had been convincing, but there was nothing to make me sure either way.

"I don't know," I said finally. "We probably won't be able to tell until we hang out with her outside of hours."

Luca shook his head. "Fat chance of that happening. She never leaves her caravan except to sit in that tent. Her mother even takes her food back there for her."

I thought of her mother's looming presence in the tent. There was something so oppressive about her, even in just the few minutes I'd spent there.

"That's a shame."

"Is it? She obviously doesn't want to be around us. Must be a stuck-up snob." Luca spat the words out. I knew his anger wasn't really about Giselle, but still it made me uncomfortable. I'd barely met the girl, but I found myself wanting to defend her.

"It's her mother," I said.

Luca made a noise in his throat. "Another stage-mum?"

I frowned. "I don't think it's that ..." I trailed off, realising again I wouldn't be able to explain it to him. There was something not right about the dynamic between them and with their tent in general. The way she was shrouded, and the whole cloying atmosphere of the candles and incense. I didn't think it was Giselle's choice to keep herself separate.

Luca shook his head. "It's this place. It makes us crazy."

I nodded. That was one thing we could agree on.

Luca stared at me, his bottom lip folded between his teeth as he chewed on it. He took a breath, but then let it go without saying anything.

I sighed. "Spit it out."

"What?"

"Whatever it is you want to ask me. I can practically see the words forming behind your tongue."

Luca chuckled and pushed my arm, gently. "You know me too well, Myra." His hand lingered on my arm. I let it for a moment, before shifting away, trying to make the movement seem natural.

"I've been saving," he said. "I reckon in a couple of months I'll have enough to get out of here."

"For a trip?"

He gave a sharp shake of his head. "No, like *out of here* out of here. Go do something else, see the world."

I frowned. "But you love performing," I said. For all his complaints, I knew deep down he had a passion for the circus. He wouldn't have run away from home to join us if he didn't.

"I do. But this isn't it."

I fell silent, unable to disagree with him. I knew the roles he'd been given didn't challenge him. There was supposed to be a level of growth and training to working here, but since the accidents, everything had stagnated.

"We could get work somewhere else. Maybe study? We could do something real."

I blinked, surprised at being included in his plans. "Something real," I repeated. I thought of the costumes I'd been making. I was good – good enough that I didn't even feel conceited saying that. With some training, maybe I could do something with that. Make costumes for movies, or work towards becoming a fashion designer.

"I don't know, Luca," I said. "What if there's nothing better out there?" Of course better things existed, I knew that. But what if those things weren't for us? Neither of us had even finished school, and who would want to employ failed circus performers?

"There has to be, Myra. There just has to be."

The desperation in his voice made a similar panic start in my stomach. I couldn't tell whether mine came from the thought of going with him or the idea of being stuck here alone after he left.

"I don't know," I said again. I had no money to travel, and I couldn't ask Luca to spend his on me. Guilt twisted in my stomach as I realised, he would. If I said yes, he would take me anywhere I wanted to go no matter how much it cost him.

Luca sighed. "Just think about it, Myra? I can't stand it here much longer."

I thought of pointing out that he could go alone, but I didn't want him to. I didn't want to lose my friend.

I nodded. "I will, but I have to get to work." I had ignored the mending pile for long enough.

I pulled myself to my feet, and he stood, too, automatically reaching out to steady me, as I wobbled.

"Don't take too long to decide, okay?" He pulled me into a hug.

I hugged him back, surprised and nervous at the gesture. The hug lasted too long, and I felt something unpleasant in the pit of my stomach.

"You're a good friend, Luca," I said. I wondered if he could hear the worry in my voice as I said that.

He sighed and let go. "Yeah."

I looked away. The unpleasant something in my stomach grew, as I realised him leaving without me wasn't the only way I was at risk of losing him as a friend.

Chapter Four

That night, I found myself once more outside her tent. There was a small gap between the curtains, and I craned my neck, trying to see through it. The candles had been blown out, and I couldn't see anyone inside. Their caravan was quiet and still too. In fact, the whole grounds were strangely silent, as if a curfew had been imposed and everyone had hunkered down for the night already.

I sighed and ran my hands down my face. What was I doing here? I needed to let go of this obsession or the spirits wouldn't be the only things causing me to fail.

"I've seen you watching."

I gasped at the voice and spun around, losing my balance. Her hand shot out, clasping my arm before I fell. Something fluttered from my stomach up into my chest. We were face-to-face, so close it was almost intimate.

She smiled, amused by my shock at having been caught peeping. The veil was gone, and her face was as soft and pretty as the blonde hair which floated around her. I had an urge to reach out and brush the strands back from her cheek.

"So, you're not blind," I said.

She laughed, a light tinkling sound, and I blushed, horrified that those were the first words out of my mouth.

"I'm sorry," I croaked, embarrassment making my throat clench. "I didn't mean–"

"It's okay, Myra. I've heard the whispers."

I swallowed. "There are always whispers here."

Her eyes narrowed a little at that, and she studied my face. I dropped my gaze, my cheeks flushing again.

I snuck looks at her. She seemed paler in the moonlight. Yesterday the candles had washed her with a warm glow, despite the dark theatrics of her tent. Tonight, she was cold and pale, her hair bleached bone-white by the darkness. It made her seem more ethereal. It was almost like I could see the spirits she spoke of swirling around her.

"I am blind," she said.

I looked up, frowning, and she laughed again at my confusion.

"Legally blind," she added. "I can see a little, but I find it hard in bright light. It's easier in the dark. That's why I don't come out much during the day and why I wear the veil."

I nodded. It was similar to my leg, I guessed. I wasn't completely paralysed – I could walk a little – but it still changed things, made them more difficult. It was easier at night when there were less people to navigate through.

"Totally blind works better for the act. It makes things more mysterious."

I nodded again, not sure how else to respond. It was as I had suspected – the fortune telling was just an act – but I couldn't help but feel disappointed to hear her admit it. She had almost drawn me into believing she was really able to commune with something beyond us. I guess I had needed to believe that. It was like Luca with his plans of leaving. We all just needed to know there was something else – something *more* – out there.

She smiled. "You're easy to see, though. You're magic."

I frowned. "I am?"

She reached up, pulling a sequin from my cheek.

I blushed again. "I work in the costume room. They're everywhere."

She smiled. "It's pretty."

My words disappeared again at that. It wasn't like she was calling me pretty, but I still didn't know how to take a compliment. She watched me, clearly amused by my inability to respond, then she moved her hand, looping her arm through mine.

"Come for a walk with me, Myra?"

We walked through the circus grounds. I thought of pointing things out to her, but she didn't seem to want a tour. I asked about her life instead, the other places she and her mother had worked. She had moved around a lot, but it all seemed much the same. Each new place meant long hours and many faces filing past, none of them making an impression. I liked listening to her talk though. She had an interesting way of looking at the world, and she made me laugh with her stories.

She asked about our circus, and I told her about the accidents; the rumours of the curse. I didn't tell her people thought I'd caused it, nor did I go into details about my fall. The evidence was obvious in my limp, even without her being able to see clearly.

She didn't repeat her words about the spirits, though I was sure they must be crossing her mind as they did mine. I wondered if perhaps she had already heard the rumours, and that's where her urgent warnings had come from. Another trick to add validity to the act. Afterall, someone must have told her my name; it wasn't a stretch to think they could have told her more.

She asked a few questions, mostly about the people who worked here. I answered as best I could, but I mostly kept to myself, so I only knew the superficial basics about the people around me. Eventually I told her as much.

"Your mother's like mine," she said.

I frowned. "I didn't–"

"You didn't have to. You're a fifteen-year-old working in a circus."

I shook my head, confused. "What does that have to do with anything?" I heard the defensive note in my voice and was surprised by its presence. I had criticised my parents many times for their choice to raise me in a circus, but it was different to hear it coming from someone else.

Giselle didn't answer. We had circled back to where we had started, and she stared at her caravan, her expression hard to read. "She won't let me out," she said quietly.

"Your mother?"

She didn't answer, but I took that as a yes.

"Because of your sight?"

Giselle made a noise in her throat. "That and other things."

I touched her arm, wanting to say something comforting but feeling unsure of what that would be. "It must be hard to be stuck inside all day," I said.

"It would be all night too, if she had her way. I have to sneak out when she falls asleep."

I shook my head, frustrated on her behalf. I thought of my mother's strained hovering each time I left our caravan. She never tried to stop me, but she made it clear she didn't think I should be going anywhere except the sewing room.

"My mum's scared of me falling if I go out alone," I said, "but she can't bear to watch me struggling to walk so she won't go with me either."

Giselle's and my disabilities were very different, but they caused a lot of the same problems. Perhaps this had been why I was sure things would change when Giselle arrived. Maybe all I really wanted was to talk to someone who understood the life I lived now.

Giselle was quiet for a moment, then she turned to face me, stepping in close to me again and taking both my hands. "Then we make the perfect pair, don't we? I'll help you balance, and you'll be my guide." She leant forward, kissing me lightly on the cheek.

I breathed in, catching the scent of incense on her hair. It didn't make me want to cough this time, it just smelt nice. My stomach fizzed with something I wasn't sure I'd ever felt before, and my face heated up again.

She let out another little tinkling laugh. "You're blushing," she said.

I noticed her cheeks were pink too and her eyes sparkled. For once I wasn't ashamed of the way my skin heated red every time I experienced the slightest emotion. I wanted my feelings to be on display. I wanted her to see them.

I leant forward, kissing her lips. They were soft, and they tasted of strawberry. The heat in my cheeks turned to burning.

I gasped and stepped back. "I'm sorry. I'm so sorry." The words rushed out, my embarrassment making them overlap.

I heard her inhale, but I didn't wait for her to speak. I broke into a limping, stumbling run, making my way as fast as I could back to my caravan.

I slammed the door behind me, leaning against it and sliding to the floor, my knee giving way. The pain in my leg screamed, and a groan escaped my lips. I had kissed her. I had kissed her and ruined any chance I had of keeping her as a friend. In the morning, I would be the gossip whispering around the grounds.

At first, I was almost glad of the physical pain. It came in waves, mirroring the embarrassment I felt and distracting me from it. But as the pain increased, it made my stomach churn and became a reminder of everything that was wrong with my life here.

I crawled up onto my bed, mortified tears leaking out and coating my face. From under my pillow, I could smell the lavender, and it made me cry harder.

LUCA SAT WITH ME AT breakfast. If he'd heard, he didn't say anything. I still couldn't look at him though. My cheeks burned so hot and so long I was sure everyone must think I was sunburnt, though that was pretty unbelievable today. The day was overcast – neither windy nor burning hot for once.

The breakfast tables were set up outside, the weather finally allowing us to eat in comfort rather than crammed between caravans, crouching low for shelter. Even so, I felt like everyone would judge the blush of my skin, labelling me from the moment they caught sight of me. I didn't raise my face for them to see. I kept my eyes on my uneaten eggs and just hoped Luca would be kind when the whispers inevitably reached him.

"No accidents yesterday," Luca commented.

I nodded, but I was well beyond caring.

"Perhaps we should start a pool, earn some money guessing who'll be next."

I nodded again. I could tell he was trying to bait a reaction from me; expecting me to either chide him for his callousness or laugh along with him, topping him with an even darker joke. But my mind was not on the falls, other than my own from grace.

"Are you okay, Myra?" He reached out, touching my hand.

I jerked my hand away, nodding. "The pain's bad today." I thought it was an explanation he wouldn't question, especially as there was truth to it. The ache from last night hadn't subsided and that, along with everything else, had kept me awake all night.

Luca frowned. "It's not just that, though, is it? I know you, Myra. What's wrong?"

I sighed. He was right, he did know me, and sometimes that was both a blessing and a curse. I studied his face, wondering how he would react.

"I did something stupid," I said finally. He was my friend, and it would be better if he heard it from me, I supposed, but it didn't make it any easier to say aloud.

"You can tell me. What was it?" Luca's brow knotted together, and he reached for my hand again.

I opened my mouth to speak, but a gust of wind rushed through the grounds, disrupting the plates around us. Luca's and my attention were drawn away, as startled chatter started up around us, and people rushed to hold down objects the wind was trying to steal.

A familiar tapping across the ground made me turn. Giselle was making her way across the grounds, her mother at her side, their arms tightly linked. The wind whipped the shawl around both of them, the tassels like tentacles, slithering their way around the two. Giselle's face was covered by the veil again, presumably to block out some of the light. It swished gently against her hair as she moved, but it still kept her hidden.

"Huh. So, they've finally come out to play." Luca had turned back as the gusts settled again. He watched them approach, his expression unreadable.

I stood, suddenly, unsure whether to run in the other direction or towards Giselle, ready to beg forgiveness.

Chapter Five

Luca was staring at me, surprised by my behaviour. He glanced from my shaking hands to the pair approaching us.

"Myra, did they do something–?"

"Giselle!" I surprised myself by shouting. She and her mother both stopped as did several other people around me. I found my tongue had now gone slack, no other words forming to explain my outburst.

Giselle tilted her head towards her mother, speaking softly, then they resumed their slow approach.

I sat down with a thump, horrified that I had just made everything even worse.

Luca put his hand on my shoulder, leaning in to speak quietly. "Seriously, Myra, what is it? What's wrong?"

I just shook my head, shame sealing my lips.

Giselle's mother led her over to our table. Giselle reached out, finding the back of the chair beside me. She slid into the seat, her incense-smell washing over me as she did.

Her mother sat down opposite. "So lovely to eat outside, isn't it? It will please the spirits greatly that we are spending time in nature."

I felt Luca's eyes on me, his smirk at her mentioning "spirits" barely contained. I nodded, still too embarrassed to speak.

"Who is at the table?" Giselle asked.

I frowned. Surely the overcast sky wasn't so bright that she couldn't see us at all? But perhaps she was not ready to admit to everyone that the blindness was in part an act. Luca was clearly waiting for me to introduce him, as I was the one who had met her already. I wasn't sure I could force words out, given how paralysed with embarrassment my tongue felt, but I opened my mouth anyway.

"Myra," I croaked. "And my friend Luca."

"Nice to meet you." Luca's face was surly, and his voice came out just as croaky as mine. He wasn't good with people when he wasn't performing; there was a reason I was his only friend here.

"Myra." Giselle's face lit with a smile. "I thought that was your voice."

The knot in my stomach eased a little. She wasn't running from me at least. That had to be a good sign.

Her mother stood. "Giselle, will you be alright alone for a few moments?" She hovered, and the overprotectiveness Giselle had mentioned felt palpable in the air.

Giselle nodded. "Myra will look after me."

Her mother headed off towards the food tables. I nudged Luca. He frowned at me, so I nudged him again.

He finally got the message and stood, following after Giselle's mother. "Let me help you," he mumbled. He glanced back over his shoulder, giving me a look which I interpreted as both "you owe me" and "you better explain later".

I mouthed "thank you" in response.

The knot had tightened again at the thought of being alone with Giselle, but I needed a chance to explain or apologise, or perhaps both. I was glad of her veil. She was sitting so close to me, and I felt like I would have dissolved had I been able to see her beautiful face right next to mine.

I kept my eyes on the table. Though I had made Luca leave in order to have this time with her, I was searching desperately for something to say but coming up with nothing. Just as I was ready to drop to my knees and crawl away in shame, I felt her hand creep under the table, reaching for mine. She found it and squeezed my fingers tight.

"I'm glad you're here," she whispered, leaning over towards me. "I spent all morning persuading Mother to let me come out, just in hopes of finding you."

I stared at her, my mouth gaping. I'd been sure she was going to ask why I'd run away last night, or worse, what on earth I'd thought I was doing kissing her.

It took me a moment to find my voice. "I ... I thought you might be mad."

"No? Why would I be mad?" Her face broke into a smile. "I'm happy."

My chest squeezed with a different kind of pain to the one I'd been carrying with me since last night. I felt like I would burst with excitement and joy, turning into nothing but sunlight and the scent of lavender.

"Ohh," was all I managed to say. My face broke into a grin though, and I was sure she would be able to feel it, even if she couldn't see it for herself.

"I forgot to ask," she said. "What did you wish for?"

"Huh?" I looked up.

Giselle squeezed my fingers, bringing me back to her. It took me a moment to remember the wish – the whole reason she had given me the lavender in the first place.

"I'm not supposed to tell you that, am I?" I said.

She laughed behind the veil. "That's just a superstition."

I had to laugh too, at the fortune teller dismissing superstitions. She definitely looked different in the daylight. She wasn't quite as magical without the ghostly paleness, but the warm sunlit glow on her hair was beautiful.

"I'd thought you might have wished for your leg to be better," she said. "But it was something else, wasn't it?"

I frowned. It was strange the way she said that – so certain – and I wondered how she knew I hadn't. Honestly, it hadn't even occurred to me to wish for that. The disability was difficult – painful – but it was a part of me now. Wishing it away would have almost seemed like a betrayal. I didn't say that aloud though. I knew she may have spent many wishes hoping for her sight to return.

"I couldn't concentrate to wish," I admitted. "After the fortune ... I just kept thinking about you." The dread that had followed me since last night came back a little at that. I couldn't see her expression behind the veil and the fear that she found my behaviour creepy started to build up again. If she hadn't been holding my hand, keeping me grounded, I think I would have run again, despite the pain it would have caused me.

But then she smiled, slowly. "Then it sounds like you got your wish." She laughed, and I joined her, delighting in the cheesiness of what she'd just said.

I'd never realised until that moment what people meant when they said their heart skipped a beat. I felt a little flip inside my chest, and the meaning was more than clear.

I tried to force myself to stop grinning as Luca and Giselle's mother re-joined us. Giselle dropped my hand as soon as her mother returned. My stomach dropped too, then I remembered her words about her mother's overprotectiveness and tried not to take it personally. It was hard when all I could think about was whether I would get to kiss her soft, strawberry lips again.

I could see Luca glancing between me and Giselle. He knew me well enough that he would have instantly noticed my change in mood. Even so, I didn't look at him or try to explain anything. He could wait. For now, I would just enjoy the light, bubbly feeling coursing through me at knowing Giselle was happy.

Chapter Six

We didn't have any plans to meet, but I sought out Giselle that night, hoping she would have snuck out of her caravan too. I hovered outside her tent, as I had done the night before, waiting.

"I hoped you'd come."

I turned at the sound of her voice behind me, and her hand was on my arm, steadying me, before I even began to stumble.

"You've got to stop creeping up on me." I kept my tone light, and I couldn't stop the smile spreading across my face, so the admonishment didn't hold much weight. I didn't want it to.

She grinned back, slipping her arm through mine. "How can I creep up on you when you're coming to find me?"

I smiled at her logic.

"Your hair's full of magic again." She reached up, pulling another sequin from my hair. She dropped it behind us, like she was intentionally marking our path. "You leave trails of it wherever you go."

Luca said the same. He said he always knew when I'd been somewhere, because I left the sparkles like breadcrumbs.

"I like it," Giselle added. "It means I can always find you, shining in the dark."

I grinned, her words warming my cheeks.

We did the same as we had the night before – walking around the grounds, talking, our arms linked; me her guide, her keeping me from falling. It was different though. A different energy coursing between us; the touches of our skin felt more charged, even though it was just the insides of our elbows meeting.

I didn't rush to kiss her again, and she seemed in no hurry to kiss me either. It didn't matter. I just wanted to be around her, to hear her stories and that tinkling laugh in response to mine.

She leaned her head against my shoulder as we walked. "Can I ask you something?"

I nodded. "Anything." I really meant that too. It felt easy to be honest with her.

"How do you feel about your leg?"

I raised my eyebrows at the question.

"Only if you want to tell me," she added.

I frowned, thinking it over. "I feel okay about it. It bothers me when it hurts, but I guess I've just got used to it now." There were things I couldn't do anymore, and sometimes that was frustrating, but mostly I didn't think about it. This had become my new normal. I'd reached a point where I was just thankful for the movement I did have, rather than aching for the bits I didn't

She chewed on her lip. "So, if someone said they could fix you, you wouldn't do it?"

I stopped and looked at her. "I don't need to be fixed, I'm not broken."

She stared at me for a moment, then we started walking again. I could almost hear her thoughts buzzing, puzzling over that. I hadn't really answered her question. If someone gave me the opportunity to have the pain go away, I think I would take them up on it, but I had made peace with the rest of it. If it were a case of reversing time, having the accident never happen, I don't know if I would do it. I liked most of my life now, and I couldn't be sure I would have ended up on the same path if it wasn't for my fall.

"How do you feel about your eyes?" I asked.

"I hate it," came the immediate answer.

I nodded, not questioning it. There had been times I'd felt like that too.

My limp became more pronounced as the pain increased. I tried to hide it, to keep moving, but after a while, Giselle stopped.

"You're hurting," she said.

I shrugged, in an attempt to downplay it. "It's okay."

She didn't answer, just waited.

I sighed. "I've been walking too much." I didn't want to admit the pain running away from her had caused, and it was true I had already been sore from my many laps around the grounds. "I can do a little, but I get tired. It starts to hurt more."

She frowned, and I dropped my gaze, not wanting to see the pity I'd seen from everyone else twisting her features, especially after the conversation we'd just had. She brushed her hand down the side of my face, making me look up. She kissed me, gently, on the lips. My stomach and chest exploded with sparks, and I felt like I was disappearing into the scent of her incense hair.

She pulled back to look at me and cupped my face in her hands. "Then we will not walk anymore." She kissed me once more and then took my hand.

She led me over to the big top. The late show was still going, music greeting us before we reached the entrance. I wasn't keen to watch, having seen it all a thousand times, but I realised it was all still new for her. I resigned myself to making that a thousand and one times, but then suddenly Giselle changed course. She led me around the side of the tent, heading to the back entrance.

We slipped inside, finding some chairs and hiding in the shadows, backstage. Giselle peered out through a gap in the scenery, watching the acrobats' routine. I wondered why she had chosen to come around the back if she really wanted to watch the show.

"Is it too bright out the front?" I asked.

Giselle was staring at something on the stage and didn't answer at first. Then she nodded. "There is definitely too much light out there ... and my mother."

"What?"

I looked through the gap. It didn't take me long to spot her mother. She sat in the audience, looking out of place still wrapped in her black shawl when everyone around her was dressed in celebratory bright colours.

"She shouldn't be here," Giselle said. Her face and her tone were both dark.

I felt the niceness of the evening we'd spent together slipping away, ruined by the pain in my leg and the pain in Giselle's side that was her mother.

I touched her arm. "It's okay, she can't see us back here."

Giselle nodded, absently. She was still watching something out the front – whether the performers or her mother, I wasn't sure. Her hand slipped into mine, though, and she squeezed my fingers.

"They're so high up," she said.

I looked through the scenery to the stage, as she pointed. The performers were balanced one on top of the other, making a dramatic human pyramid. It was nothing compared to the heights I used to fly through on a daily basis, but my stomach still clenched. The girl at the top wobbled slightly, making micro-adjustments to counter the movements of the others below her. I knew the deal – knew it was all perfectly normal and under control – but the tension in my body still built at the seemingly precariousness of her position. I felt myself start to sweat. Her image blurred, double-vision-induced ghosts dancing around her. I realised I was dizzy and looked away.

I tried to meet Giselle's eye, to give her a cue that I wanted to leave, but she stared at the performer, transfixed. I suspected I could wave my hand in front of her face, and she would just keep staring. It was a look I'd seen many times. If you didn't know the way things worked behind the scenes, much of the circus was mesmerising.

I watched Giselle's mother instead. She held herself tightly, her gaze also fixed on the performer at the top of the pyramid. Her jaw was clenched, all the tension I felt displayed on her face too. She said something to herself, whether a prayer or an incantation I wasn't sure.

"Your mother–" I started to say, but a gust of wind interrupted me. It rushed against the side of the tent, blowing it into us. I caught hold of Giselle, and we braced each other.

I heard a scream, a sickening thud. "No!"

Giselle's gaze was still fixed on the point where the performers had been, but her mouth had dropped open in horror.

I turned, not wanting to see the crumpled body I knew would be there, but something forcing me to look anyway.

Suddenly, she snapped out of it. "We shouldn't be here!" She grabbed my face, not letting me look. "Come on." She pulled me from the tent.

There were more screams now. The other performers surrounding the fallen girl, and audience members rising from their seats, unsure what to do. In the middle of it, I could see Giselle's mother just standing there, still whispering to herself. I stared at her, over my shoulder, as Giselle pulled me away.

It was too far away to be sure, but she seemed to stare straight back at me.

I WAS STILL SHAKING when we got back to Giselle's caravan. We'd run the whole way, both of us stumbling as Giselle struggled to see the path, and I tried to ignore the pain blaring in my bones.

We stopped, both heaving as we gasped in air, trying to catch our breath.

"It's okay, Myra, it's okay," Giselle was saying.

"She fell!" I realised I was saying it over and over.

I'd heard people gossip about the falls; Luca had told me about each one. But this was the first one other than my own that I had seen. I found I was laughing, a strange, humourless, hysterical sound.

Giselle held my face, kissing my cheeks and my lips, in a panicked attempt to calm me. I laughed more at the irony of that.

"It's okay," she said again. She started to laugh too, until we were both holding each other, nervous giggles working their way through us.

I leaned my head against her shoulder. "Do you think she'll be okay?" I asked.

The question sobered both of us up a little.

Giselle gave a firm, single nod of her head. "She will. She wasn't hurt badly, I promise."

I nodded too, trying to reassure myself. I had fallen from far higher, and I was okay, I told myself; in pain, but still okay.

Giselle had gone quiet, and her grip on me had changed. It felt less desperate now. More like she was holding me because she wanted to, not because she had to.

I moved my head, so I could look at her. She held my eye, and my fear dissipated. I felt safe in her gaze.

"I'm glad you came out tonight, Myra," she said. "I ... I like being with you."

She sounded shy, for once being the less confident of the two of us. It made the fluttering feeling start up in my chest again.

"I like being with you too."

In the distance, we could still hear the commotion caused by the fall. I felt some guilt at my happiness now, but I knew that on the night I had fallen there would have been couples sharing moments as I was rushed to the hospital. In every day, there were so many different mini worlds overlapping each other. We couldn't always feel each other's pain, just as we couldn't always share each other's happiness.

Giselle sighed. "I better go inside. My mother will be back soon."

I frowned, thinking of how Giselle's mother had behaved during the girl's fall. There was something not right about it, but I shook the feeling off. Giselle didn't need to know about my imagined fears.

"My mother ..." Giselle paused, biting her lip, and for a moment I thought she had read my thoughts. "We mustn't say anything in front of her – about us."

My stomach dropped, and I knew my hurt must show on my face, but Giselle rushed to continue.

"Not because of you, I mean. Just because I'm not supposed to be outside. She would be mad if she knew I was sneaking out."

I nodded and sighed. Mine would be too, I realised. We were not children, but sometimes our disabilities made our parents think we were. I wondered how my parents would react to my growing feelings for Giselle. Somehow, I thought they would be happy for me – the fact that Giselle was a girl wouldn't make a difference, I didn't think. But they would only be happy once they accepted I was old enough to date at all. My mother wasn't ready to do that, and it was clear Giselle's wasn't either.

"This will just be for us, then," I said.

A smile broke across her face, and she kissed me. "Just for us," she said.

Chapter Seven

It carried on that way for the next couple of weeks. During the day, I felt shut out of Giselle's life. She either avoided me completely by staying locked inside her caravan, or when she did venture out, she kept up the blind act, which made it harder to feel close to her. I couldn't relax around her when she was pretending to be someone else; at least not the way I could at night.

I tried not to take it personally. My stomach dropped each time she looked straight through me, but her mother's presence during the day gave a clear explanation for why her behaviour was so different. I still wasn't sure what I'd seen just before the performer fell, or if I'd seen anything at all. Something didn't feel right, though. I wasn't sure how much Giselle knew – or didn't – so I kept quiet regardless.

My evenings with Giselle made up for the daytime weirdness. When we'd both finished for the night, and everyone else was occupied with the late performances, we would slip out and I would come find her, waiting in the shadows by the fortune telling tent. Then, just like she had said that first night, I was her guide and she kept me balanced. In more ways than one, I realised. The nights with her made the long days sewing and the pain from my accident easier to bear. My father even commented that I seemed happier, that I was smiling more. My mother's shoulders relaxed a little at that, as if some of the guilt had slipped away.

There had been more accidents, though. I didn't know many of the details, I'd just heard the rumours. Some said they saw ghosts around people just before things went wrong. That frightened me. It's what I'd seen before the girl fell from the pyramid – ghostly double images dancing around her as my eyes blurred. I told myself it was a coincidence and pushed that idea to the back of my mind, but it lingered there, not letting me ignore it completely.

The girl from the pyramid wasn't hurt too badly – two sprained wrists and a concussion. She hadn't returned to work though. A few other performers had left as well, claiming the curse was more dangerous than it was worth. My parents hadn't mentioned it, but I noticed they spent little time in our caravan now, presumably filling in for the missing acts. Luca probably would have been able to tell me exactly who was gone, but I'd been avoiding him. I felt bad for it – I knew how much my friendship meant to him – but I had never been able to keep secrets from him, and I wasn't ready to share this one yet. His friendship meant a lot to me too, but I needed time to explore what was happening between me and Giselle, and I hoped he would understand that.

Giselle and I never spoke about the falls. I'm not sure if she'd heard about them – she didn't really spend time with anyone other than me and her mother. I could have told her, but I didn't want to spoil the nice safe space we had built between us.

Over the nights, she explained some of her fortune telling methods to me. "I used to watch their body language," she told me. "Most of the time you can tell pretty quickly what it is they're wanting to hear. That works best for the good fortunes, then when they ask for a full, you just have to throw in a couple of warnings. Usually about strangers and taking risks."

I laughed, realising that's almost exactly what she'd said for me. "How do you do it now? When you can't see their body language."

She smiled. "Get them talking, mainly. Listen for tiny changes in their pitch, the smell of sweat when they get nervous." She squeezed my hand. "And I measure their pulse rate, when I take their hands."

I glanced down and saw her finger had slid to the vein on my wrist without me noticing. "That's very clever."

"It's sneaky, I don't know that it's clever." She sighed. "Of course, the spirits help me too. Whispering things I need to know when the time is right."

I looked up at her. Her face was serious, no hint that she was being facetious, but she had to be, didn't she? She had told me it was all an act.

"Why did you say that, about the spirits wanting to claim me?" I felt cold, remembering the fear her words had laid on me at the time.

"Huh?" She stared at something in the distance in front of us, either ignoring or oblivious to my puzzled stare.

"When you told my fortune. You said they had taken a liking to me ... Then something about us needing to fight them or we would all fall."

The words seemed darker, given the accidents. Even knowing that her fortune telling was all an act, I couldn't help but see it as having been an ominous premonition.

Giselle frowned as I spoke. There didn't seem to be any recognition in her face, and I wondered if she remembered saying it. If I was more given to superstition, I would have thought perhaps the spirits had taken her over to speak those words. She was staring intently into the middle distance, the way she had just before the girl fell the other night. Her hair seemed even paler. Wisps of it floating around her face like cobwebs, drawing attention to her colourless cheeks and the dark circles under her eyes.

"Are you okay, Giselle?" I asked.

She turned to me, blinking, as if she'd forgotten I was there. I looked towards where she had been staring. A figure was watching us, shrouded in a shawl. If it was her mother, Giselle had to know that, even with her weakened sight.

"La Lune," she said.

"What?"

"That was your final card, wasn't it? La Lune – the moon." She glanced up at the full moon above us.

"I think so. I don't remember." I shivered, despite the warmth of the night.

"The card of deception and trickery."

I looked from her to the figure in the distance. She said it like it was supposed to mean something to me, but it seemed stupid when the whole reading had been an act of deception and trickery.

I wondered what her mother wanted by following us. Giselle had said her mother would be bothered by her sneaking out, but she was making no move to come after us, simply standing and staring. I started to wish she would come over –

drag us both back home – just to get it over with. Her presence in the distance was giving me chills.

"Is that a playground?" Giselle asked suddenly.

I followed Giselle's eye to the playground just outside of the circus ground. "Yeah, there's one on the other side of the fence."

Giselle smiled. "We should go."

"To the playground?" I squinted. I could barely see the play equipment myself; I wasn't sure how Giselle had managed to spot it. I glanced back at her mother, but Giselle avoided looking that way again.

She took my hand. "Let's pretend we're children again."

Part of me wanted to press her. To ask what was really going on between her and her mother. There was more to it than just the desire to keep her inside at night, that much was obvious. But Giselle bit her lip as she waited for me to answer, and I found myself nodding.

"Okay, let's go."

I let her lead me to the fence, then I took over, showing her where there was a gap we could squeeze through.

She ran over to the swings. "Come on, I'll push you!" She laughed, sounding happy and childlike.

I followed her, reluctantly.

She was light on her feet, dancing, too excited to stay still. "Come on, Myra!"

I sat down in the swing, though my stomach twisted at the thought of it. "How did you see the swings, Giselle?" I asked.

She pushed me into the air instead of answering. I leaned back, bending my legs on the backwards swing to build the momentum.

She seemed so confident in her steps tonight, no hesitating or checking the ground ahead was stable, and she had run right to the swings. I wanted her to give me an explanation – to tell me that she had seen the light glint against the metal chains of the swings or that she had been here before and mapped out the playground in her mind.

"Go higher, Myra!" she shrieked, laughing. She pushed me harder, sending the swing wobbling towards the sky.

An unpleasant thought crept its way into my mind. Perhaps the legal blindness was an act too, a lie on top of a lie. I stretched my legs out, trying to slow the swing, but she pushed me again, sending me shooting back up.

Why, though? Why would she pretend to have limited sight, when she had already admitted to me that she wasn't totally blind? My stomach jolted as I hit the top of the swing's arc and started to fall. I stretched out my legs again, hoping to catch the ground on the way back, but it suddenly seemed very far away.

The circus was full of con people – in a way, it was our job. You might think there would be a code of honour against duping each other, but you'd be wrong. We were all so used to gaining the trust of strangers and breaking it just as easily. It was a hard habit to quit. Her blindness was what made me trust her.

I hit the top of the arc again and felt the sickening drop in my stomach as I fell back to earth. "Giselle, I want to stop!" Panic made my voice rise. I twisted around, trying to look at her, but that just made the swing wobble and shoot higher. "Giselle!"

Her tinkling laugh floated back to me. "No, go higher, Myra. Go all the way to the sky! Fly up and we'll be stars together." She pushed me again, sending me shooting back up.

"Please, I want to stop!" In the distance, I saw the cloaked figure. "Giselle!" I shrieked. "Let me off!"

I grabbed the swing's chains, making it jerk dangerously back and forth. I lurched forward, getting my feet on the ground, but my leg gave way. I scrambled forward, looking for her mother's figure in the distance.

Giselle had stopped, frozen with her hand on one of the swing's chains. She stared into the distance. No, not into the distance. She was staring at her mother, transfixed like she had been the night the girl fell from the pyramid.

She suddenly snapped out of it, coming back to herself. "Myra?" She stumbled forward, the hesitant steps returning as she tried to find me. "I'm sorry, I thought you were joking."

I looked back to where her mother had been. The figure was gone, having left now I was on the ground. Perhaps that's what she'd wanted all along – for me to fall again.

"Myra?" Giselle reached for me, her soft, beautiful face scared, taking on my panic. "I'm so sorry, I should have known the swing would scare you after your accident."

I took her hand, helping her find her way down to the ground beside me. She cupped my face, peering into my eyes, trying to calm me.

I felt my breathing start to slow. Of course – my fall. The swings mimicked the sensation of dropping through the air. That was why I felt panicked, and why I had started to have doubts.

Up close, I could see her eyes were unfocused, darting back and forth much quicker than eyes normally did, as she tried to see me properly. It wasn't an act. Her new confidence had come from me – from us – and I had just trashed that.

"I'm so sorry," I whispered.

She folded me into her arms and held me.

SOMETHING CHANGED AFTER that night. Giselle and I still met up each evening, and I still loved spending time with her, but the ease of the first few weeks we'd spent together was gone.

Her mother's figure haunted us. Giselle became jittery every time she was near, though she still acted like she didn't realise we were being followed. I didn't press the issue, wanting to avoid the confrontation, but my fears and suspicions about what her mother wanted grew. The accidents continued, and though I couldn't prove anything, I felt like she had something to do with them.

Another figure had started to follow me too – Luca. I saw him every day at meals, or when I ventured down to the smoko area. But after a few minutes, I would make up an excuse to get away from him.

We were friends, and I tried not to make it obvious I was dodging him, but I knew he must be suspicious. I wasn't quite sure why I hadn't told him what was going on. It was obvious Giselle's mother knew now, so there was no real reason to keep up the secrecy. I just couldn't get past the feeling that things would change between me and him, once the news was out.

Of course, things were changing between us anyway. He stopped approaching me, knowing I would disappear on some flimsy pretext if he did. Instead, he was just always there, everywhere I went, on the edge of my peripheral vision, trying to catch my attention.

It was unkind of me to keep avoiding him, I knew that, so when I saw him hovering nearby one evening as I waited for Giselle to finish her last fortunes of the day, I waved him over.

"Luca," I called. "Come sit with me."

He hesitated, perhaps thinking I would change my mind and walk away before he reached me. "Hey, Myra. I feel like I haven't seen you in days."

"That's because you haven't." I grinned. "Been busy. So many new costumes." It wasn't a lie, there had been a lot of work in the costume room, altering outfits to fit replacement performers as more and more people left. I still felt my cheeks flush at my lie by omission.

"Oh ..." Luca's posture softened. "That's good. I thought you were avoiding me."

I looked down at the ground, scuffing my feet in the dirt.

"Because I asked you to come with me, I mean," he added.

I'd forgotten about Luca's plan to leave, and his offer to take me with him. With everything else going on, it had completely slipped my mind.

I'd been undecided before, but now with things between me and Giselle, there was no way I could go. I opened my mouth to tell Luca as much, but then I stopped. I wasn't quite ready to tell him about Giselle, and I didn't know how else I could explain my rejection of his offer.

His face fell, before I managed to say anything. "You're not going to come," he said.

I dropped my gaze. "I'm sorry, I can't."

"Your parents would understand, Myra." He took my hand, squeezing it. "I promise."

He was wrong, they wouldn't, but that wasn't the point.

I shook my head again. "Luca, I–"

He touched my shoulder, interrupting me and making me look up. He had a sparkle in his hair, a rogue one that had migrated from my unruly locks to his. I reached up to brush it away, but he misinterpreted the gesture. His hand slipped from my shoulder to my cheek and he kissed me. I froze, surprise and confusion overwhelming me for a moment.

Then I pushed him away. "Don't!"

His face fell. "I thought ..."

I couldn't look at him. "I love you, Luca. You're my best friend, but–"

He looked away, not letting me finish. This is what I'd been afraid of, I realised. I'd tried to ignore it, but I'd known how he felt. I'd known that if I told him about Giselle, I might lose him.

"It's not you, Luca, it's–"

"Don't, Myra." He shook his head, still not looking at me. "You don't need to pull out the platitudes." He stood, not quite walking away from me, but putting distance between us. His cheeks were burning in a way I'd felt on my own skin many times, embarrassment taking over him.

"No, you don't understand." I stood, clumsily, reaching for his arm to balance against. "It's really not–"

He shook his head again and started to back away, moving out of my reach. "Please, just don't."

"Luca ..." I leaned against the caravan instead, frustrated by my inability to follow after him. In a second, I would find my balance, the pain in my leg easing, and I would be able to walk after him. But in a second would be too late.

"I'll talk to you later, Myra."

He walked away, and I had to let him. I wanted desperately to explain about Giselle, to make sure he knew it really *wasn't* about him, but I could see he needed time. I hoped I wouldn't lose him as a friend, but I wasn't sure I would be able to control that. In all honesty, I'd known for a while how he felt, and I'd known I didn't feel the same. But it had taken Giselle arriving to show me why.

"What was that about?"

Giselle stood behind me, watching Luca walk away. I didn't understand how she managed to creep up on me every night. I was beginning to think she was doing it on purpose, just to watch me jump.

I shook my head, not ready to talk about it. "Nothing, it's not important." My cheeks flushed at that lie. It was very important, but only to me and Luca.

Giselle frowned, and her lips pinched together. I wondered how long she had been listening. Something about her expression told me she had heard the whole thing. I waited to see if she would ask, but instead she held out her arm for me to link through.

We walked around the grounds as usual. My leg was still sore from getting up too quickly, so we took it slowly. Giselle was strangely quiet though, and she was holding herself tightly.

I found myself growing tense too, drawing discomfort from her. I knew I should tell her exactly what happened, to clear the air, but I couldn't bring myself to do it. I felt bad for Luca and it seemed like a breach of trust to discuss his embarrassment further.

Giselle paused across from the big top, staring. Luca dangled from a bar set above the entranceway. As people entered, he'd steal hats from their heads and other simple pranks before they noticed him. To anyone else, the performance would have looked as it should, but I knew him too well for that. He was distracted, his mind wandering, and his movements were slower than usual, everything a beat late. I cringed internally, knowing I was where his mind was wandering to.

Giselle frowned as she watched.

"Giselle ..."

She didn't look at me. The wind picked up around us. The dirt swept up and seemed to dance in the air. Summer was coming to a close, but it seemed the strange, hot winds would be following us into the fall.

I sighed. "You saw what happened, didn't you?"

"You kissed him." She still didn't look at me.

I shook my head. "It wasn't like that. He kissed me, and I pushed him away."

"But you said you love him."

The wind dropped away again, but the bits of dirt still seemed to move, swirling in patterns around us. Giselle's hair swirled around her too, the strands wafting across her face.

"I love him as a friend, Giselle. He doesn't know about you. You wanted us to keep it secret."

Giselle made a noise in the back of her throat.

"I don't mean it like that. I'm not blaming you. I just mean..." What did I mean? It wasn't Luca's fault, but I could still understand why Giselle was hurt. From her point of view, he had crossed a line. One he didn't know existed, but it was there nonetheless, and his kiss had breached it.

I went to brush the strands of hair back from her face. They swirled away, my hand seeming to go straight through them. I frowned. The dirt was still shifting, patterns appearing and disappearing around us, and her hair seemed to do the same. She had an aura of colours around her, ghostly double images, just like the others had before they fell. I stepped back as I felt dizzy.

"Giselle?" I said again.

She looked at me, her eyes shifting away from Luca for the first time. She held my eye for a moment, then she gasped. "My mother," she said.

I turned. Her mother was standing outside the big top, watching us. I reached automatically for Giselle's hand, wanting to comfort her. She squeezed mine tightly, her nails biting into my skin.

Her mother didn't approach, just stared at us. The wind picked up again, and it seemed to focus on her, whirling in circles around her. It changed as it did, becoming opaque. I stared, open mouthed as white wisps of wind wrapped themselves around her, until she was bound tightly by them. She clenched her fists at her sides – trying to fight or control them, I wasn't sure.

She looked from us to Luca, dangling in the entranceway. And then he screamed.

"Luca!" I started forward.

I didn't see him hit the ground, the crowds hiding that from view, but I heard the collective gasp as it happened.

I turned back to Giselle, knowing I couldn't leave her to find her own way home. She studied my face for a moment. I was sure she would see my fear and guilt written across it – fear for my friend and guilt that my rejecting him had been the distraction that made him fall. I hoped she could also see how much I cared for her, and that none of my feelings about Luca changed that.

"Go," she said. "My mother will help me get home."

I nodded. "Thank you."

She touched my face, gently running her hand down the side of my cheek. I kissed her lightly, then limped over, pushing my way through the crowds surrounding Luca.

Chapter Eight

I didn't go out to meet Giselle the next night. I just kept seeing Luca's face in my mind, his hurt written across it. Was it my fault he fell? I should have told him about Giselle earlier. He was my best friend, and I should have told him.

He'd landed on his head and had a concussion. That's all I knew. The medic team had pushed me away, not letting me stay by his bedside. If it had been a day earlier, Luca probably would have insisted I stay with him. I would have happily been the one to look after him, to wake him every hour until he was out of danger. As it was, he didn't acknowledge I was there nor protest when I was asked to leave.

The sound of his scream kept playing over and over in my head and there was something else niggling at the back of my mind, but I couldn't quite face it. The way the wind had changed around Giselle's mother, I had to wonder how much she was controlling. She had looked at Luca just before he fell.

The colours and patterns that had floated around Giselle weren't normal either. I had dismissed her talk of spirits as part of the act, but it was getting harder and harder to do that. I thought of the rumours that people had seen ghosts dancing around the performers before they fell – I'd seen it myself, just before the girl from the pyramid dropped to the ground. I wondered if the ghosts I'd seen around Giselle meant the next accident would be hers. I cut that thought short before it could fully form.

My spiralling thoughts were interrupted by a knock at my caravan door. I hesitated, wondering if I could pretend to be asleep. It would likely be someone coming to give me news of Luca's state and I wasn't sure I could deal with hearing it.

"Myra? Are you in there?" Giselle called.

I got up, opening the door. "Giselle, how did you get here?"

She gave that tinkling laugh. "I walked, of course."

I wrapped her in a hug, so glad to feel her warmth against me. "I meant how did you see to get here? You shouldn't be wandering alone, it's too dangerous."

She laughed again. "You sound like my mother."

I pulled back to look at her. She didn't seem to have any hesitation at mentioning her mother, no guilt or fear around it. Perhaps she hadn't seen what I had. The wisps of wind were so light and flighty, easily missed even with perfect sight. I shook my head, questioning again whether they were only in my mind.

"I had to come," she said. "You didn't come to me."

I felt a pang of guilt at that. She was right. I had waited outside her caravan every night since we met. She must have been confused to find me missing, but I just hadn't been able to face going out when things had gone so wrong last night.

She touched my face. "You've been crying."

I nodded, bowing my head as I felt like it was going to start again.

"Why?"

I looked up at Giselle, frowning. How could she need to ask that? We had watched Luca fall. She had seen him make his feelings clear and me reject him. She must surely know how much it had hurt us both.

"Because of Luca, of course."

She stared at me, her expression hard to read. Was she still upset by the fact that he had kissed me? It seemed so trivial now, so unimportant when he was injured.

She smiled. "You need a distraction." She took my hand, trying to pull me out.

I kept my feet planted, letting my arm stretch between us. "No, I can't ... my mother said I can't." I flushed at the lie; my cheeks giving me away as usual.

Giselle went still, dropping my hand. I wrapped my arms around myself, familiar shivers working their way up my body.

"So, both our mothers are trying to pull us apart now."

Her tone was cold, and I didn't like the hardness to her voice. Again, the image of the wisps surrounding her mother came into my head. There was something really wrong here, and Giselle getting caught in it scared me.

I stepped out into the night, taking her hand again. Whatever else was going on, the feeling of having her close to me still felt right. "Okay, let's go out," I said. "But just for a little while."

GISELLE INSISTED SHE had a surprise for me. I let her lead me through the night. My misgivings hadn't settled. It felt wrong to be wandering around so freely when Luca was hurt. But Giselle pulled on my hand and chattered as we walked, keeping me distracted.

She led me into the big top, a skip in her step.

I hesitated. Everything was closed down for the night – the late performance cancelled due to the number of performers absent. I wasn't sure we were allowed to be in here after hours, especially after all the falls.

"Giselle, I don't think–"

She took both my hands. "No questions. This is my surprise."

She led me inside, then skipped away from me. Her steps were surprisingly confident. I realised her arm hadn't been linked through mine all night, and she'd made her own way over to my caravan. I felt the same doubt I'd felt in the playground. I tried to push it away again. Her confidence was growing perhaps, her feet having learned the way through the grounds. The doubts refused to be quashed. I was happy to see the ease with which she moved, but it still left me nervous and confused.

"Close your eyes," she called.

I frowned. "Why?"

Her tinkling laugh echoed around me. "Because it's a surprise."

I sighed, then closed my eyes, covering them with my hands to make it clear I was following her wishes.

"Good girl. Now, don't peek until I say."

I waited, a feeling of dread growing with every second. There was a rustling sound and then nothing. "Giselle?" I called.

She didn't answer. Outside, I could hear the wind picking up, a low rumbling starting as it caught the sides of the tents.

"Giselle?" My voice was squeaky with anxiety. I dropped my hands, not waiting for an answer.

I couldn't see her. I spun on the spot, looking for her.

Her tinkling laugh rung out from above me. "Naughty girl, Myra. I told you not to peek."

I gasped. She was halfway up the ladder, climbing up to the trapeze platform.

"Stop! What are you doing?!"

She turned to look at me, her foot stepping into nothing as she missed a rung.

"Giselle!"

How could she have found the ladder, let alone managed to climb the steep rungs? She laughed, finding her footing and leaning back dangerously. She didn't seem like herself, a wild energy taking over her.

"What are you doing? Get down from there!"

"No, my love, you come up here." She was still laughing, like it was nothing. Was this a punishment? Was she mad about Luca and risking her life in order to make me feel bad about it? She was far too high already but still climbing.

I found I'd moved to the base of the ladder and was staring up at her. "Giselle ..." I hadn't been up there since the day of my accident, the thought of doing so making me ill. Even the swings had terrified me. If I was honest, the reason I couldn't watch my parents' routine wasn't just that I was bored with it. Every time they flew through the air, it made my stomach clench.

"Please come down, Giselle."

"No, you have to come up and get me." She leaned back again, watching me.

"Why are you doing this?" I whispered the words, but she heard them anyway.

"You need to face your fears, Myra." Her voice lilted, turning sing-song. "Come up here and face them." She let her foot dangle as she peered down at me.

This was insane. She sounded drunk, or crazy, or … something. Whatever it was, this wasn't my Giselle.

"Myyy-raaa," she called. She leaned her head back to give me an upside-down grin. Her other foot slipped from the rungs, and she swung forward, slamming into the ladder. She shrieked as she was left dangling by her hands.

"Giselle!" I found I was climbing, having started up without thinking about it. "It's okay, I'm coming!"

"Myra, hurry!" The laugh was gone from her voice, terror taking over.

I reached her quickly, climbing up behind her. I wrapped my arm around her, bracing her so she could get her feet back on the rungs. She was crying, shaking and sobbing, in no state to climb back down.

"Keep going," I said. We were nearly at the top. If we reached the platform, we would have time to rest and for me to calm her down.

"I can't!" She wailed, her tears turning to hysteria. She flopped back against me, nearly causing us both to fall.

"You can!" *You have to*, I added inside my head. "I'm right here, Giselle, just keep climbing."

She took a shuddering breath, then stepped up onto the next rung.

"That's it! You can do this."

She was shaking badly and so was I, but I moved with her, my hands and feet just one rung below hers, matching each step. She reached up, her hand touching the platform. She let out another shriek when she couldn't find a rung.

"It's okay! You're there. Just climb up."

"I can't!" She cowered, clinging tighter to the rungs.

"Shh, it's okay. I've got you." I climbed up over Giselle, reaching the platform myself and clambering up onto it.

She grabbed my wrist. "Myra! Don't leave me." Her face was even paler than normal, terror written across every part of her body.

"I'm not; I won't." I gripped her arms, guiding her up onto the flat surface. "You're okay, Giselle."

She crawled towards me and I held her, letting her cry against me. Thoughts were swirling in my mind, trying to put together what was happening. The pieces were all there, but I couldn't make them fit properly.

"What the hell were you thinking?" I whispered.

"I wanted to help you." Giselle shook her head back and forth, as if she were trying to erase what had happened. "I thought if you came up here again, you wouldn't be so afraid."

I stroked her hair. "It doesn't work like that."

"I know, I'm sorry. I'm so sorry."

"Shh, it's okay." I wanted to believe her, but so much of tonight didn't make sense. The doubts I'd had about her blindness were no longer just doubts. I cupped her face, pulling her away from my shoulder so I could look at her properly. "You're not blind, are you?" I asked.

She didn't answer, just stared into my eyes. As she did something seemed to change. My eyes blurred, and she split into two, the double-vision induced ghost very real suddenly. I dropped my hands, scooting to the other side of the platform.

"Please don't be afraid, Myra," she whispered. Marks appeared on her face, little silver lines like cracks. "I thought love would be enough, but they wanted fear."

I couldn't form words. I looked down at the platform. It was littered with sparkles already, shaken from my loose hair. Within seconds, I had left my trail.

"You never have sequins on you," I said.

"What?"

I looked up at her. "I leave them everywhere, but I've never seen one stick to you."

I heard a noise below us, someone entering the tent. I turned, expecting to see her mother, stalking us as she had all the nights before. Instead, the figure I saw below was haloed in soft blonde hair, her veil-covered face angled up towards us.

"Giselle?" I turned back, looking from the girl in front of me to the one below.

I screamed. The Giselle on the platform with me covered her ears. I blinked and the one below disappeared, but I screamed again. The world tilted, and I clung to the platform, certain I was falling.

Giselle grabbed hold of me, her arms wrapping around me trying to comfort or kill me, I wasn't sure which. "Shh, they get stronger with fear. I'm so sorry, Myra. I'm so sorry. I'm sorry."

She kept saying it over and over, and I kept screaming, unable to do anything else. I pressed my face into the platform, doing anything I could to avoid seeing the way her form was splitting.

I felt the vibrations of someone else climbing the ladder to the platform, but I couldn't look. It would be the second version of her; the veiled one. I couldn't bear to see the two of them closing in on me with no escape but to jump.

"Myra? Myra, it's me."

I heard the voice and felt the hands shaking me, but I couldn't look.

"What's wrong with her? Why are you up here?"

It was Luca's voice. I opened my eyes, but I couldn't make myself turn and look. They were playing tricks on me. She and her mother were in it together.

"I brought her here." Giselle's voice was shaking. "I thought it would help."

Luca made a noise in the back of his throat, his anger at hearing that obvious. "Myra, come on, please. It's me; it's Luca." He lifted my shoulders gently, turning my face towards him.

His face was bruised, a cut crusted in dried blood at his hairline, but it was him. I risked a glance at Giselle. The cracks on her face were gone, and there was only one of her, but I still shuddered as I remembered the way she had split in two.

She stared at me, her lip still shaking. A tear made its way down her cheek. She shook her head, in what seemed like a desperate attempt to communicate silently with me.

"I'm so sorry," she said again.

She reached for my hand, but I cringed away, not wanting even the slightest contact with her.

Luca sniffed then cleared his throat, his discomfort clear. It wasn't fair that he was having to rescue me, when I'd hurt him, but right now I needed him.

"How did you know we were up here?" Giselle asked, her voice low.

He shook his head. "I couldn't sleep, I was walking. Heard you both screaming."

I covered my mouth, feeling another scream building up at the memory. Luca's face pinched up with worry as I did.

He shifted, moving towards the edge of the platform. "Let's get you down from here, eh?"

Giselle visibly flinched at the idea of climbing down, and I felt myself do the same.

"Okay, okay." Luca responded to our unspoken protests. "We'll go slowly, one at a time."

He took Giselle down first. I stayed huddled on the platform as they made their slow descent. He climbed behind her as I had done on the way up. I didn't watch, just waited for the vibrations of the ladder to stop, signalling that they were on the ground safely.

I heard their muffled voices at the bottom, but none of the words were clear. I was glad. There was nothing either of them could say that would make sense of this. I felt Luca start his ascent, then his head appeared over the edge of the platform.

He squinted slightly, assessing my position, still curled up in a ball, my arms locked tightly around my legs.

"You ready?" he asked.

I nodded but didn't move.

"I won't let you fall, Myra."

His words would have meant more, if he hadn't just fallen himself, but somehow, I still trusted him. I scooted over to the edge and let him guide me back down to the ground.

Giselle wasn't waiting at the bottom.

"She said she had to get back to her mother," Luca said, when he saw me looking around.

I nodded. I wasn't sure whether I was relieved or just confused by her absence. I knew I would have to unravel what had happened, but none of it made any sense. I started to cry again, thinking of how she'd been fooling me. Did she ever really care for me, or had that been an act too?

Luca touched my shoulder, then wrapped his arms around me when I didn't stop. "What the hell happened tonight, Myra?"

I shook my head, unable to speak.

"Are you and Giselle ...?" He let the question hang without finishing it.

I nodded, though I wasn't really sure what we were now. I wasn't sure what she was.

He let out a breath. "Wow." He started to laugh then stopped when he realised I was still crying.

"I'm sorry, it's just ... wow."

He walked me back to my caravan. My leg was so sore, I had to shuffle, leaning heavily on the arm he wrapped around me. I could see he had questions, but he had the sense not to ask them tonight. His mood was lighter though, the tension from after he kissed me gone. I was glad he understood now – knew for sure that it wasn't about him. I just wished it hadn't come as a result of whatever it was that had happened tonight. We stopped outside my door.

"Myra ..."

He glanced back towards the big top, and I couldn't help a shudder working its way up my body.

"Is everything okay?" he asked. "Between the two of you?"

I shook my head. "No. It's really not."

Chapter Nine

The next day, I stood outside the fortune teller tent for far too long. I didn't go in – only partly because of the crowds. Instead, I watched as she told fortunes, still swaddled in those layers of fabric.

Her words echoed in my mind: *I thought love would be enough, but they wanted fear.* There was fear everywhere now, as we all waited for the next accident. We were cursed, even the most sceptical of us couldn't deny it. Or if it wasn't a curse, there was something else unnatural here, and I had a feeling it was too late to fight it.

"Did she tell you how she lost her sight?"

I started at the sound of Giselle's mother's voice. Her hand shot out, just as Giselle's had, steadying me. She withdrew it as soon as I was stable. I could still see the wisps around her, though they were fainter in the daylight. They circled her slowly, keeping her trapped in a tiny, translucent prison.

"Did she tell you?" she repeated.

I shook my head, my throat too tight for words.

"It was an accident." Giselle's mother's voice held the same sadness my mother's did on the rare occasions she spoke about what had happened to me. "At one of the other circuses we worked at. There was an explosion. She was the closest to it. She hasn't seen a single thing since."

I thought of telling her mother that I knew Giselle could see, but she was so determined to keep up the act, it seemed pointless to try dissuading her from it. Besides, after last night, I had to question whether I really knew anything about Giselle at all.

"That must have been very hard for both of you," I said instead. There was an edge to my voice – not quite sarcasm, but a hardness I'd never heard from myself before.

"Oh, it was, it was. Giselle was very angry for a long time. Kept talking about negligence and revenge. She took it very hard and it made her bitter."

I frowned, unable to find anything sensible to say to that. I shifted my weight, stretching out my leg. My muscles were tight, and I was still moving slowly after last night. I ached for an arm to link through, a shoulder to lean against.

Giselle's mother watched my movements. "I'm glad she's met you, Myra. The way you handle your ... affliction." She gestured towards my leg. "It's good for her to see."

I wasn't sure about that. I had made the best out of my situation, taking as much joy in my new role in the sewing room as I could. But it was still hard.

"I'm glad I've met her too," I said. "I ... care very much for her." Even after everything, that was true. I wouldn't have been there, waiting outside her tent, and trying to figure out what on earth was going on, if I didn't.

"Yes, it's clear you are very special to each other." Her mother smiled, and I wondered if she knew exactly how much we meant to each other. The thought made me nervous though, as I realised I wasn't sure that was what I wanted anymore. A similar tension had crept into her mother's face.

Her mother sighed. "The spirits have helped her. She turned to them eventually, of course." Giselle's mother's face turned pinched. "But perhaps they have helped her too much," she said quietly.

Her fingers curled, in and out, making fists as she had the other night when I'd seen the webs wrapping around her.

"What do the spirits look like?" I surprised myself with the question. I'd barely made the connection myself before the words were out of my mouth.

Her mother looked up, puzzling over the question. "It depends," she said finally. "Most people don't see them at all."

I dropped my gaze, feeling my cheeks start to heat.

"But ... something tells me you do." She whispered the last part, fear crossing her face.

I nodded, slowly.

"Wisps, mostly. Changes in colour and light – moving patterns."

I thought of the strands of hair that always floated around Giselle's face, the ones I hadn't been able to brush away. And the cards, the way the designs had changed and swirled.

"Where have you seen them, Myra?" Her voice had dropped low, the quavering note she normally affected gone completely, as she became serious.

"Around you." I swallowed. "And Giselle. I thought you were causing them at first." I didn't tell her about how I'd seen her watching us. After seeing the veil-covered girl below us last night, I was pretty sure it had been Giselle all along.

"They're wrapped around me, aren't they? Binding me." She nodded to herself, not waiting for an answer. "Sometimes they are stronger. Sometimes they take the shape of a person. But the copy is not the same. It's–"

"Paler," I said, my stomach dropping. "More ethereal."

Giselle's mother nodded, tension written across her face as she read into what I was saying.

"Tell me honestly ..." I swallowed, having trouble getting the words out. "Is Giselle really blind?"

Her mother hesitated, a slow breath rattling against her teeth. "Completely," she whispered. "She can't see a thing."

I thought you might have wished for your leg to be better. I remembered her words, and suddenly I understood them. She had made a wish too – she had wished for her eyes to be better. I had wished for her instead, whether I meant to or not, and we had both been granted what we'd asked for.

I looked back at the tent. Giselle sat at the table, the veil over her eyes. Her skin and hair were warm, bathed in the yellow of the candlelight. Her hair fell softly around her face, no wisps or stray white strands.

She was the figure I had seen watching us. She had been following us, as the pale spirit form and I had fallen in love.

I thought love would be enough, but they wanted fear. There was still more fear to be had at the circus. There was still more potential for falls.

I turned and limped away as fast as I could. The pain in my leg screamed, but I forced myself to keep moving.

"I'm sorry, Myra. I'm so ..."

I heard her mother calling after me, but I didn't stop.

NOW THAT I KNEW WHAT to look for, I could see them everywhere. Wisps, like cobwebs or stray pale strands of hair, danced over everything – over everyone. It was no wonder so many had fallen. They wrapped themselves around all the performers, stretching between their limbs like tripwires.

I found Luca at the smoko spot. "Luca," I called.

He smiled, stepping towards me, but his face fell as he saw the fear on mine.

"Please, Luca, I need your help."

"What is it, Myra?" The bruises on his face had deepened overnight, and I could see him wince as he spoke, the words causing him pain.

"It's her. Giselle. I think she's causing the falls."

He shook his head. "What?"

"There's two of her ... I think. But one of them is a spirit. The spirits are everywhere. They wrap around people, and–"

"Myra!" My name came out draped in a laugh. "What are you talking about? You're not making sense." The amusement on his face started to drop, being replaced with concern, as he realised I was serious.

He was right, it didn't make sense. I knew that. But I also knew it was true. She had been growing stronger. It had been happening right in front of my eyes, but I hadn't wanted to see it.

"Please, Luca." I gripped his hands. If Luca didn't believe me, then no one would. "You have to trust me."

He frowned, clearly torn. I had broken some of his trust, and this had to be confusing for him. But he knew me – knew me better than anyone else, and he had to know I wouldn't make this up.

His expression set into one of grim determination. "What do you need?"

"I ... I don't know." I cut myself off. I had no plan. Worse than that, I had no idea what Giselle or the spirits that had taken her form were planning either. All I knew was that they were trying to cause fear.

I could see Luca's frustration was growing, my lack of explanation confusing him further.

"The big top," I said finally. "I think that's where she'll be."

The main tent hadn't yet opened for the morning show. My parents were inside, rehearsing a new routine. My mother swung back and forth, building up the momentum to leap into my father's arms. I knew better than to call out to them, not wanting to disrupt their concentration, but I had to get them down. I could see the spirits snaking their way around their limbs, just waiting for the right moment to make them drop.

"They're everywhere," I whispered.

The white wisps were sneaking their way around Luca too. He couldn't see them, but I think he could sense them. He scratched at his throat as they wrapped around it, and his manner grew more urgent.

He stared up at my parents. "We should get them down."

I nodded, glad he was cooperating. "I don't want to distract them, though."

He made a noise of agreement. "I'll climb up, tell them you're sick or something."

I touched his arm. "Thank you." I could see he still didn't entirely understand why we were doing this, but I was glad he trusted me enough to realise it was important.

He gave me a half smile, then he was off. I watched as he climbed the ladder to my dad's platform. I hoped my parents would listen. They were meticulous about their rehearsals, letting very little interrupt them. But Luca could be convincing when he wanted to be, and I hoped this was one of those times.

I cringed as my mother finally leapt. But my father caught her wrists, their hands locking on to each other. He grinned at her, his strong arms holding her, as he had held me many times. I let out a breath. They were safe for now.

Something caught my eye up on my mother's platform. The wisps seemed to be congregating there, swirling around a figure dressed in white.

"Giselle," I whispered.

I didn't give myself time to think. I limped over to the ladder and began to climb.

I hadn't noticed the pain when I climbed up to save Giselle. My focus had been on her, and the adrenaline covered everything else. This time it was difficult, my knee didn't want to bend enough to reach the rungs, and a sharp pain stabbed each time I forced it. My leg started to shake, threatening to give way, but I bit my lip and kept going.

Giselle didn't turn around as I reached the platform. Spirit-Giselle, that was. The other was still back telling fortunes. She knew I was there, though. The wisps fanned out from her, circling me and drawing me to her.

"It wasn't meant to be like this," she said.

I swallowed, feeling like I couldn't breathe with the wisps surrounding me. "How was it meant to be?"

"I just wanted to be able to see again."

I shook my head. "You're not her. Stop pretending, I'm not stupid."

She spun around, grabbing my arms and latching on to them. "I am, Myra. It's me! Don't you understand?"

I stepped backwards, the momentum of her sudden movement nearly sending us both flying off the edge of the platform. She pulled me to her, steadying me and protecting me from falling. I leaned my head against her shoulder. The familiarity of her embrace was too much for me. I wanted to just melt into it, forget everything that had happened. But I couldn't.

I pulled back from her. "You're not real. You're one of those spirits." My voice cracked as I said that. I wanted desperately for her to tell me I was wrong, but instead she started to cry.

Across from me, I could see Luca had reached the other platform and was talking to my parents. They were safer now they were off the ropes, but I would rather they were on the ground. I could see Luca was having trouble persuading them to come down.

"I just wanted to be able to see. They gave me a way to do that through them. But it's still me in here. They've given me the form, but it's still me!"

Giselle reached for my hand and I took it automatically. I wanted to believe her. Maybe she wasn't like the spirits that coated everything. She seemed different – more in control than the random way the wisps floated around things.

"I didn't mean for any of this to happen. I thought I could stop the falls."

I stepped closer to her, brushing the white strands away from her face. Of course she had tried to stop them. I knew her, she was good. She wouldn't hurt people.

"The spirits needed emotions to fuel this. To give me another form." She leaned her head against my shoulder. "When I met you, I thought our feelings would be enough."

I nodded and pulled her closer to me. My feelings for her were the most powerful emotions I'd ever felt. Without her having to say it, I knew it was the same for her.

"But they still wanted fear," she whispered.

Something sank in my stomach, and I pulled back. "You can't let this continue, Giselle. You can't let anyone else fall." I glanced over to my parents and Luca. They were still on the platform.

She gripped me tighter, her nails digging into my skin. "But don't you see, Myra? I'm getting stronger. It's nearly over."

I frowned. "What do you mean?"

"That day on the swings, I realised what I needed for this to be permanent." Her face lit up, her eyes becoming wide and manic, like they had been when she was on the ladder climbing up the last time. "I needed *your* fear. The spirits have craved it since you fell."

"What are you talking about?" I stepped back, but I was on the edge, nowhere for me to go. I looked for Luca. He and my parents had caught sight of us and were frozen, watching.

Giselle's face turned serious. "Oh no, my love. You don't need to worry. I won't hurt you. I couldn't." She ran her hand down my face, but I flinched away. "But I saw how afraid you were when Luca fell. When *I* nearly fell."

I shook my head. "Giselle ..."

Tears leaked from her eyes again. "Please don't think I'm callous, Myra. I don't do this lightly."

A gust of wind rushed through the tent, and my mother screamed. She overbalanced, but my father and Luca grabbed for her. My father fell instead. He seemed to hang in mid-air. I screamed, rushing forward as if I could fly through the air and save him. But then he hit the ground. Giselle grabbed me, holding me back.

She pressed her face into the back of my shoulder. "I'm sorry, Myra, I'm so sorry."

I stared down at my father's broken body then spun around, anger seething through me. I wanted to hit her, to claw at her face and make her feel the pain she had just caused me. But something in her face stopped me. The silver cracks were appearing across her skin again.

She sank down to the platform, covering her face with her hands. "No, no, no!" She shook her head back and forth. "I'm so sorry, Myra. I can't control it anymore. The spirits are taking over."

I turned back, staring down at my father's body. I was shaking, and a wailing sound was filling the air. I wasn't sure whether it was coming from my mother or from me.

"I wouldn't have done that. I wouldn't have hurt anyone, you know I wouldn't!"

I didn't know what to believe. The wild look I'd seen on her face, it wasn't her, it wasn't the Giselle I knew, but right now I couldn't be sure I'd ever really known her. It was all so mixed up – what was her, what was spirit?

"I want to stop, but I can't," she whispered.

Another gust of wind rushed through, and Luca was knocked from the platform. He caught the side of it and dangled by his hands from the edge.

"No!" I turned to climb down, but she was blocking my way.

"I'm sorry, Myra, I'm so sorry!"

The wisps floated around her, creating a haze. They were feeding from her, growing stronger. I did believe her, I realised. She was split by this. The spirits gave her strength, but they also took it from her.

She reached for me. "Believe me, I didn't want this."

Luca and my mother both screamed as the platform tilted. It shouldn't be able to do that, but the wisps were wrapped so tightly around it, manipulating everything.

"Please stop this, Giselle."

She stared up at me. "I would if I could," she whispered.

I heard a gasp from below. I turned. Giselle's mother stood in the middle of the tent, the white-veil-covered Giselle beside her, their arms tightly linked. The girl looked weak, growing fainter as the spirit-Giselle's strength grew.

"I tried to fight them, but I failed," the veiled-Giselle said from below me. "Now, we will all fall."

The wisps crowded around them. Giselle's mother clutched at her chest. She looked like she was having a heart attack, but the white tendrils creeping around her hand showed the truth. They were killing her, their malice given full flight now.

"Giselle, you have to stop this!" I wasn't sure which one of them I was talking to. Both perhaps. The veiled one stood helpless, while the spirit girl in front of me switched between crying and a wide-eyed manic stare that told me the wisps were taking over.

"There have to be more falls, it's the only way." She stood, joining me at the edge of the platform.

We watched as my mother and Luca scrambled, clinging to the platform as it bent unnaturally. I looked from her mother's gasping form to my father's broken one down on the ground. Finally, I looked to the veiled-Giselle, as she sunk to her knees beside her mother. The wisps were circling her too, smothering and weakening her. She raised her head, pleading with me, from behind the veil.

The spirits wouldn't be done. They may give Giselle back her sight, leave her in this new form after killing the old one. But that wouldn't be the end of it. They would attach to someone else. Split and twist them until they became something they weren't. Cause them to do unspeakable things, preying on their sadness.

"Yes, there needs to be another fall," I said. I turned and pushed Giselle from the platform.

Chapter Ten

Her mother didn't make it, and neither did my father. Giselle was fine though. The "real" one, I mean, though it felt wrong to call her that when the other had meant so much to me. The spirit-Giselle had broken apart in the air, dissipating into wisps before she hit the ground. My mother had pulled Luca to safety, and we had all climbed back to the ground, too shaken to speak about it.

I still couldn't process that my father was gone. I felt numb instead of grieving, though perhaps that was part of the process. My mother hadn't spoken about it, or about anything. She had sat silently in our caravan since it happened.

The real Giselle was leaving. I don't even know who I heard that from, it just seemed to be collective knowledge. I debated whether or not to go see her. In the end, I realised I had to, or it would haunt me forever.

She was sitting outside her tent, and it seemed like she'd been waiting for me. She had her veil on, but she raised her head when I approached.

I hovered beside her, unsure whether to sit or stay standing. A few days ago, I would have wanted to be as close as possible, but now the comfort and familiarity of being in her presence were gone.

"Le Chariot, La Roue De Fortune, Le Diable, L'Amoureux, La Lune ..." she said.

It took me a moment to recognise the words. "The cards. But–"

"I couldn't read them, no. But the spirits told me."

I remembered her warnings. I was so caught up in being with her, there was no way her words could have reached me. Would things have been different if I had taken the warnings seriously? I didn't think so. There was no way I could have predicted that the spirits would take her form.

"Do you know what they mean?" she asked.

I shook my head. "No."

She patted the ground beside her, gesturing for me to sit. I hesitated, then lowered myself to the ground beside her. Her arm brushed against mine, and even with everything I knew now, I still felt butterflies in my stomach.

"The Chariot – trouble, upset, change." She spoke as if reading from a textbook, listing each of the cards and their meanings. "The Wheel of Fortune – destiny involving great gain or great loss. The Devil – reversed – physical or spiritual release, overcoming handicaps, enlightenment. The Lovers ..." Her voice cracked, and she took a long breath. Despite myself, I found I was reaching for her hand. She squeezed mine, and I started to cry.

"The Moon – a warning against false friends, deception and trickery." She paused, letting me process all of that. "It was all there in the cards," she said. "I just couldn't see it. The reading was meant for me, not you."

"You tried to warn me." My voice rose, turning that into a question. I wanted her to reassure me that she had. I wanted her to say she had at least tried to stop it.

"I did." She nodded, reassuring herself as much as me, it seemed. "But the spirits needed your fear to gain power. They needed the falls."

I stretched out my leg, easing the pain in it. "But the accidents ... they started well before you arrived."

She moved her hand, playing with my fingers, then she shrugged. "Your fall ... it really was just an accident. Nothing more, nothing less. But the spirits attached to you after it, like I said. They were already here when I arrived, causing mischief. I gave them something else to focus on." Her voice didn't hold any shame for what she'd done. All the people who had gotten hurt, it was like none of us even mattered.

I dropped her hand. "You made a wish, didn't you?"

She nodded. "I didn't realise until it was too late what it would cost me to take that form."

"So, none of it was real?" I couldn't bring myself to say it properly – the feelings, the kisses we'd shared – none of it had really been her. The spirits had wanted me to feel, so they'd tricked me into thinking they were her.

Giselle hesitated, then slowly she removed her veil. Underneath, her face was scarred, a web of silvery lines scattered over her eyelids. Her eyes themselves were bloodshot and unfocused.

I looked away, blinking as tears beaded in my eyelashes. I wanted to hate her, but she was still just as beautiful as she had always been. She was still the girl who had made me fall in more ways than one.

She touched my arm, but I couldn't look at her. "She was a way for me to have freedom again." The spirits were still wrapped around her, the wisps binding her tightly the way they had her mother. She thought they had given her freedom, but really they had imprisoned her.

I sniffed, hard, trying to stop myself from crying. "You were just using me." I didn't make that a question, and I didn't need a confirmation from her.

The energy and the spirits attached to me from my fall had fuelled her freedom. I understood the desire for independence. Every time my leg gave way, or pain kept me indoors, I wished desperately to escape the confining barriers of my life. The accidents we'd had and the consequences of them were hard, but it didn't excuse what she'd done. She didn't have the right to mess with people's lives – with my feelings – in the way she had.

She reached out hesitantly, finding my face with her fingertips. "Everything she felt, I felt it too. She was me. It was real, Myra."

I wanted to believe that she'd felt the same way I did, but even if it were true, it didn't matter. She may have cared for me, possibly even *loved* me but she had still used and hurt me.

"That's not enough," I said.

She swallowed, the sound audible in the quiet between us. She dropped her hands and shifted away.

I waited with her until one of the workers came and told her he was ready to go. He was giving her a lift to her aunt's place across the city. He treated her with kindness, believing her to be the poor, unfortunate, disabled girl, grieving her mother. There would be no consequences for her, other than losing the spirits that had enabled her to roam at night through them. Half of the circus workers had no idea what had happened, still telling themselves the accidents were just a horrible coincidence. The other half – the superstitious ones, and the ones who had seen too much of what happened last night to dismiss it – knew what she had done, but there was nothing any of us could do about it.

She paused before getting in the car. "Goodbye, Myra. I wish ... I wish I had met you earlier – before I made the wish to see again. I ... I think things might have been different if I had."

She leant forward, offering a final kiss.

I didn't lean in myself. "Maybe they would have."

She hesitated, still waiting, then when I didn't return the kiss, she got in the car and closed the door. I watched them drive away, feeling grief for the girl I'd thought I'd known mixed in with grief for the others we had lost.

LUCA WAS WAITING BY my caravan, a packed bag at his feet. I slowed my pace as I saw him. He'd told me not to take too long to decide whether or not I wanted to go with him. I'd delayed, and now the decision was made for me.

"So, you're leaving too." I couldn't keep the reproach from my voice.

"I asked you to come with me." His tone sounded harsh, but the sulky look on his face told me he didn't mean it. He was sad, not angry.

"I couldn't say yes, Luca."

He surely had to understand that now. I could see how he felt about me, and it wasn't fair to let him think things would have changed if we'd run off together.

"No, you couldn't have." He stared at me for a moment then stepped towards me, taking my hands. "But you can now."

I felt my eyes widen, a flicker of the hope I'd lost returning, but it was fleeting. I shook my head. "Just because of what happened with Giselle, it doesn't change ... how I feel. I still like girls, Luca."

He gave a wry smile. "She's not the only girl in the world, Myra." He paused, studying my face. "And neither are you."

I dropped my gaze, embarrassed again for not being honest with him from the start. "I'm sorry," I whispered.

He shook his head. "You don't have to apologise. I love you, but you can't love me back. That's just the way it goes sometimes."

I took his hand. "I *do* love you. Just ... as a friend."

Luca frowned, his face pained for a moment, then he squeezed my hand and put his arm around me. "Me too. And as your friend, I want you to come with me."

I met his eye and held it. He was offering with absolute honesty. There was no hidden agenda, nothing he wanted from me other than my company and friendship. He couldn't love me in the same way Giselle did, nor I him, but he would love me honestly as a friend.

"Yes," I said. "I want to come with you."

I THOUGHT OF SNEAKING out without telling my mother. Perhaps leaving her a goodbye note or calling her from the road. Instead, I faced up to it and told her I was going.

She went still at my words. "With Giselle?" she asked.

I shook my head. "No, not after what she did. Luca and I are leaving."

She nodded slowly. "He's a good boy. Always been a good friend to you."

I was surprised by her lack of protest. I'd been sure she would try to lock me away, still deluding herself into believing I would one day return to join her flying through the air.

"The circus will probably close," she said, nodding to herself. "Your father and I were one of the only things keeping it together." She started to cry at that, finally beginning the grieving she needed so badly to do.

I wrapped my arms around her, crying too. But after only a few minutes, she brushed the tears from her cheeks, moving away from me.

"I have something for you," she said. She opened her bedside drawer, taking a bracelet from it. She clasped it around my wrist. "Your father gave me that. I think he would want ..." She trailed off, emotion choking her voice. It was engraved with a single word – *Fly*.

She took my face between her hands, meeting my eye for the first time since I fell. "I love you, Myra. You call and check in with me every day, okay?"

I nodded, my turn to be silenced by emotion.

WE LEFT THAT NIGHT, hitching a ride with another one of the workers who was heading across the city to see his family. My mother was right – the way people were leaving, the circus wouldn't be around for much longer. We couldn't take responsibility for that though.

We didn't have a plan. Luca had some friends he thought might let us stay with them. Beyond that, we had only vague dreams of what we would do.

Luca closed his eyes and took a deep breath as we drove away from the circus. "Can you feel it?" he asked me.

"Feel what?" I was sitting tensely, my bag clutched on my lap.

Luca took it from me, placing it by his feet so I could sit more comfortably. "The spirits are releasing us."

I nearly laughed and reminded Luca of all the sceptical comments he had once made. I could feel it though. Like little whispers across my skin, they were letting us go, peeling back and allowing us to breathe deeply for the first time in a long while.

I thought of Giselle, and how tightly they had been wound around her. I wondered if she would ever escape, or if they would forever be tempting her, offering her promises they could only ever fulfil with fear. I hoped at least this time she would choose better. I hoped she would choose to live the life she had now instead of forever wishing for the one she had lost.

"What are you thinking about?" Luca asked.

I glanced at him, wondering how to explain. "I'm thinking I'm glad I chose to come with you," I said.

And I was. Whatever the future held for us, I was glad I was living this life, with my friend by my side.

I opened the window and let the air rush against my face. It was different from the wind that had plagued us – fresher. I shook my hair out into it, watching as sequins and sparkles flew from it, leaving me to fly back to the circus where they belonged.

Enjoyed this book? You can make a big difference.

REVIEWS ARE THE MOST powerful tool when it comes to getting attention for my books.

As an indie author, it can be hard to get my books into the hands of readers, but honest reviews help me do just that.

If you've enjoyed this book, I would be very grateful if you could spend just a few minutes leaving a review (it can be as short as you like).

Thank you very much!

Also by Helen...

BROKEN SILENCE

A stranger just put Kelsey's boyfriend in a coma. The worst part? She asked him to do it.

Seventeen-year-old Kelsey is dealing with a lot – an abusive boyfriend, a gravely ill mother, an absent father, and a confusing new love interest. After her boyfriend attacks her in public, a stranger on the end of the phone line offers to help. Kelsey pays little attention to his words, but the caller is deadly serious. Suddenly the people Kelsey loves are in danger, and only Kelsey knows it. Will Kelsey discover the identity of the caller before it's too late?

UNDERWATER

Bailey has a lot of secrets, and a lot of scars, both of which she'd like to keep hidden. Unfortunately, Pine Hills Resort isn't the kind of place where anyone can keep anything hidden for long.

When Bailey arrives, she just wants to get through summer quietly, spending as much time in the water as she can.

Then she meets Adam.

Bailey's not looking to make friends, but Adam isn't easy to ignore. Neither is his ex-girlfriend, Clare.

As Bailey grows closer to Adam, she draws Clare's animosity. Will Bailey be able to keep her past a secret, or will Clare discover and reveal the sinister truth about how Bailey really got her scars?

SYMBOLIC DEATH

A woman finds a Death Curse symbol scratched into the soap scum around her sink.

A young boy watches his family fall apart after the death of his father.

A butterfly chrysalis hatches under the watchful eye of a hungry cat, and a teenage grim reaper's job is made harder by the boy who can see her.

Symbolic Death is a collection of sad, poignant, and darkly funny tales about death. If you like unique points of view, heart-breaking moments, and a touch of black humour, then you'll love Helen's short story collection.

Buy the ebook or paperback now or get it for free by joining Helen's mailing list at www.helenvfletcher.com.

Acknowledgements

A huge thank you goes out to K.M. Robinson and Elle Beaumont. I never would have thought of setting a story in a circus but writing for the Cirque de vol Mystique anthology was the perfect challenge and encouragement. This story wouldn't have been created without you.

Another huge thank you to Stuart Bache, all the cover design students, and the SPF team. Your encouragement and feedback were invaluable in creating my first self-designed cover.

Finally, thank you Jess for your endless patience in looking at covers, blurbs and sentences I can't get quite right. You are the sanity that lives outside my body. I don't know what I would do in moments of decision-paralysis without you.

Also by Helen Vivienne Fletcher

Jenny No-Knickers
Aunt Kelly's Dog
Do Fruit Worry About Getting Fat?
Symbolic Death
We All Fall

Watch for more at https://www.helenvfletcher.com/.

About the Author

Helen Vivienne Fletcher has worked in many jobs, doing everything from theatre stage management to phone counselling. She discovered her passion for writing for young people while working as a youth support worker, and now helps children find their own passion for storytelling through her creative writing business, Brain Bunny Workshops.

Helen is the author of three picture books for children, one short story collection, and two young adult novels. She has won and been shortlisted for several writing competitions, including making the shortlist for the 2008 Joy Cowley Award, and in 2015 she was named outstanding new playwright at the Wellington Theatre Awards. Helen's poetry and short stories have appeared in various online and print publications, and she regularly performs her spoken word pieces around Wellington.

Overall, Helen just loves telling stories, and is always excited when people want to hear or read them.

You can find Helen at www.helenvfletcher.com or connect with her on Facebook.

Read more at https://www.helenvfletcher.com/.

www.ingramcontent.com/pod-product-compliance
Lightning Source LLC
Chambersburg PA
CBHW030754110726
47900CB00008B/2603